Christopher Marlowe's The Rich Jew of Malta: A Retelling

David Bruce

Published by David Bruce, 2022.

This is a work of fiction. Similarities to real people, places, or events are entirely coincidental.

CHRISTOPHER MARLOWE'S THE RICH JEW OF MALTA: A RETELLING

First edition. July 16, 2022.

ISBN: 979-8201038236

Written by David Bruce.

Table of Contents

CAST OF CHARACTERS...1
THE PROLOGUE...3
CHAPTER 1 | — 1.1 — 5
— 1.2 — 12
CHAPTER 2 | — 2.1 — 27
— 2.2 — 30
— 2.3 — 33
CHAPTER 3 | — 3.1 — 50
— 3.2 — 52
— 3.3 — 54
— 3.4 — 58
— 3.5 — 63
— 3.6 — 65
CHAPTER 4 | — 4.1 — 67
— 4.2 — 75
— 4.3 — 81
— 4.4 — 84
CHAPTER 5 | — 5.1 — 89
— 5.2 — 93
— 5.3 — 97
— 5.4 — 99
— 5.5 — 100
APPENDIX A: NOTES | Cast of Characters: Barabas 105
The Prologue..107
— 1.2 — 108
— 1.2 — 109
— 2.1 — 110
— 4.2 — 112
— 5.2 — 113
APPENDIX B: ABOUT THE AUTHOR 114
APPENDIX C: SOME BOOKS BY DAVID BRUCE..................115

Dedicated to Carl Eugene Bruce and Josephine Saturday Bruce

***

Educate Yourself
> **Read Like A Wolf Eats**
> **Be Excellent to Each Other**
> **Books Then, Books Now, Books Forever**

***

In this retelling, as in all my retellings, I have tried to make the work of literature accessible to modern readers who may lack some of the knowledge about mythology, religion, and history that the literary work's contemporary audience had.

Do you know a language other than English? If you do, I give you permission to translate this book, copyright your translation, publish or self-publish it, and keep all the royalties for yourself. (Do give me credit, of course, for the original retelling.)

I would like to see my retellings of classic literature used in schools, so I give permission to the country of Finland (and all other countries) to buy (or get free) one copy of this eBook and give copies to all students forever. I also give permission to the state of Texas (and all other states) to buy (or get free) one copy of this eBook and give copies to all students forever. I also give permission to all teachers to buy (or get free) one copy of this eBook and give copies to all students forever.

Teachers need not actually teach my retellings. Teachers are welcome to give students copies of my eBooks as background material. For example, if they are teaching Homer's *Iliad* and *Odyssey*, teachers are welcome to give students copies of my *Virgil's* Aeneid: *A Retelling in Prose* and tell students, "Here's another ancient epic you may want to read in your spare time."

CAST OF CHARACTERS

Male Characters

Machevil, the Prologue.

Barabas, the rich Jew of Malta.

Ferneze, Governor of Malta.

Selim Calymath, Son to the Emperor of Turkey.

Callapine, a Pasha (high-ranking Turkish official).

Don Mathias, Friend to Don Lodowick. In love with Abigail. "Don" is a Spanish title.

Don Lodowick, the Governor's Son. Friend to Don Mathias. In love with Abigail.

Martin del Bosco, the Spanish Vice-Admiral.

Ithamore, a Turkish Slave to Barabas.

Friar Jacomo.

Friar Barnardine.

Pilia-Borza, a Thief in league with Bellamira.

Two Merchants.

Three Jews.

Female Characters

Abigail, Daughter to Barabas.

Katherine, Mother to Mathias.

Bellamira, a Courtesan.

Abbess.

Minor Characters

Nuns, Knights, Officers, Pashas, Turks, Guard, Slaves, Messenger, Carpenters, Attendants.

Scene: Malta.

NOTES:

Machevil is the spirit of Niccolò Machiavelli, author of *The Prince*. From his name we get the adjective "Machiavellian." The name "Machevil," a version of the name "Machiavelli" that was used in Renaissance England, suggests "Make evil." People of the time believed that Machiavelli's ideas were immoral and that he was an atheist.

Barabbas was released to the Jews instead of Jesus in Matthew 27:15-26. Jesus was then crucified. Barabbas is described as a murderer in Mark 15:7 and Luke 23:19, and as a thief in John 18:40.

The name "Pilia-Borza" comes from the Italian *pigliaborza*, which means "pick-purse" or "pick-pocket."

The name "Bellamira" is *"bella mira*," which is Spanish for "beautiful — look!"

"Selim" is the name of a son of Suleiman the Magnificent, who ruled Turkey during the 1565 siege of Malta, which the Christian defenders won.

The play was first published in 1633, and the title on the title page is *The Famous Tragedy of the Rich Jew of Malta*. These days, the title is usually *The Jew of Malta*.

The Knights of Malta are the Knights of Saint John of Jerusalem. In 1530, King Charles I of Spain, who was also King of Sicily, allowed them to settle on Malta, where they established their headquarters. Earlier, the Knights of Saint John of Jerusalem had their headquarters on the island of Rhodes, but in 1522, after a siege, the Turks conquered the island.

In this culture, a man of higher rank would use words such as "thee" and "thy" to refer to a servant. However, two close friends or a husband and wife could properly use "thee," "thy," "thine," and "thou" to refer to each other.

Words such as "you" and "your" were more formal and respectful.

The title "sirrah" was used to refer to a male of lower status, such as a servant or a slave, than the speaker.

Turkey is a country in which Islam is the majority religion.

THE PROLOGUE

Machevil says this to you, the reader:

"Although the world thinks that Machevil is dead, yet his soul has only flown beyond the Alps, and now that the Duke of Guise, leader of the 1572 Saint Bartholomew's Day Massacre in which Catholics murdered Huguenots, aka French Protestants, is dead, Machevil's soul has come from France to view this land of England and frolic with his friends, devotees of *The Prince*."

People of Christopher Marlowe's day believed that Machiavelli's ideas had been adopted in France after travelling from Italy, and they hoped that those ideas would not reach and be adopted in England.

Machevil continued, "To some perhaps my name is odious; but such people as love me guard and protect me from the tongues of my enemies — or they themselves do not mention me. Let them — my followers, and my detractors — know that I am Machevil, and I don't value men, and therefore I don't value men's words.

"Admired and wondered at I am by those who hate me most. Although some speak openly against my books, yet they will read me and thereby attain to Peter's chair — the Papacy — and when they cast me off and abandon what I have taught them, my ambitious followers poison them.

"I regard religion only as a childish toy and trifle and hold that there is no sin but ignorance. Birds of the air will tell of murders past? I am ashamed to hear such fooleries."

Machevil was referring to such stories as this: Robbers murdered the ancient Greek poet Ibykos in the 6th century B.C.E. Before dying, he exclaimed to the robbers that some birds — cranes — nearby would be his avengers. The robbers laughed at him. When the robbers entered a city later, one of the robbers saw some cranes and shouted, "Look — the avengers of Ibykos." This aroused the curiosity of the citizens of the city, who — after investigating and discovering that the robbers had murdered Ibykos — put the robbers to death.

Machevil continued, "Many will talk of title to a crown, but what right had Julius Caesar to the empire?"

Machevil admired Julius Caesar for seizing power.

He continued, "Might first made kings, and laws were then most sure when, like the notoriously severe ancient Greek lawmaker Draco's harsh and draconian laws, they were written in blood.

"Hence comes it that a strong-built citadel commands much more than letters and literature — such as *The Letters of Phalaris* — can import: If Phalaris had only observed this maxim, he'd never bellowed in a bronze bull because of great ones' envy."

Phalaris was a cruel ruler of the city Agrigentum in Sicily. He commissioned Perillus to construct a hollow bull of metal to be used as an instrument of torture. The victim was placed inside the bull, and then the bull was heated. As the victim roasted, the victim screamed. Phalaris ordered that the bull be constructed in such a way that the screams of the victims sounded like the bellowing of a bull.

After the craftsman Perillus constructed the bull — something that he ought not to have done — Phalaris made him the first victim to be placed in the bull and roasted. This is poetic justice. Additional poetic justice occurred when Phalaris was overthrown and also became a victim in the bull.

If Perillus had a redeeming feature, for most people it would be his love of letters and literature, but Machevil regarded that love as a defect: Better that he work to retain power than to study letters.

Machevil continued, "Let me be envied and not pitied by the poor petty people!

"But whither am I bound — what did I come here to say? I come not to give a lecture here in Britain, but instead to present the tragedy of a Jew who smiles to see how full his moneybags are crammed, which money was not gotten without my means.

"I crave only this. Honor the rich Jew of Malta as he deserves, and let him not be the worse received as a guest because he favors — resembles and sides with — me."

Readers are unlikely to be inclined to like Barabas, the rich Jew of Malta, because of Machevil's recommendation. In fact, if Barabas is the kind of person Machevil likes, readers will be inclined to dislike him.

CHAPTER 1
— 1.1 —

Barabas was in his counting house — a place for working on his business accounts and storing his treasure — with heaps of gold before him.

He said to himself, "So in this venture thus much profit was made. A third part of the Persian ships was enough for the venture to be summed and satisfied — tallied up and paid off."

Two-thirds of the money he had received from his venture was profit; the other one-third covered his expenses.

He continued, "As for those Samnites and the men of Uz who bought my Spanish oils and wines of Greece, here have I pursed their paltry silverlings — silver coins each worth a Jewish shekel. Damn, what a trouble it is to count this silver trash!

"May the Arabians continue to fare well — the Arabians who so richly pay with ingots of gold for the things they bargain for. A man may easily in a day count those gold ingots that may maintain him all his life.

"The needy servant who never fingered a groat — a small silver coin — would consider that many silver coins a miracle, but he whose steel-barred coffers are crammed full, and all his lifetime has been tired, wearying his fingertips with counting small silver coins, would in his age be loath to labor so, and for a pound to sweat himself to death.

"Give me the merchants of the Indian mines who trade in metal of the purest kind. Give me the wealthy Moor, who in the eastern rocks — the Arabian Desert — freely and without restraint can pick his riches up and in his house heap up pearls — precious stones — like pebbles. He gathers them for free and sells them not individually but by the gross weight: bags of fiery opals, sapphires, amethysts, orange-red gems, hard topaz, grass-green emeralds, beauteous rubies, sparkling diamonds, and seldom-seen costly stones of such great price that one of them, impartially valued and of a carat of this quantity, may serve in a time of calamity to ransom great kings from captivity.

"This is the merchandise wherein consists my wealth. And therefore I think that men of judgment should arrange their means of business away from the vulgar trade, and as their wealth increases, so enclose infinite riches in a little room.”

Barabas was talking about treasure stored in a small space, but Christian believers used “infinite riches in a little room” to refer to the unborn Christ in the Virgin Mary’s womb.

Stepping into the street outside his counting house, Barabas continued, “But where is the wind now blowing? Into what corner points my halcyon’s bill?”

In this culture, people would use the body of a halcyon — the bird known as the kingfisher — as a kind of weathervane, hanging it up in a place where the wind could blow against it.

He continued, “Ha! To the east? Yes — see how stands the weathervane! East and by south: southeast. Why, then I hope my ships I sent for Egypt and the bordering isles of Cypress and Crete have reached the Nile’s winding banks.

“My argosy — my large merchant ships — from Alexandria, laden with spice and silks, now under sail, are smoothly gliding down by Candy shore — along the coast of Crete — to Malta, through our Mediterranean Sea.”

“Candy” was “Candia,” which the Italians called Crete.

Hearing a noise, Barabas said, “But who comes here?”

A merchant arrived.

“What is the news?” Barabas asked.

“Barabas, your ships are safe,” the merchant said. “They are riding at anchor in the Malta roadstead — the harbor — and all the merchants with all their merchandise have safely arrived, and have sent me to learn whether you will come and pay their way through customs.”

“The ships are safe, you say, and richly laden with goods?” Barabas asked.

“They are,” the merchant confirmed.

“Why, then go tell them to come ashore and bring with them their bills of entry,” Barabas said. “I hope our credit in the custom-house will serve as well as if I were present there. Go send them sixty camels, thirty mules, and twenty wagons, to bring up the wares.

“But are you master of a ship of mine, and is your credit not enough for that?”

“The customs duties alone come to more than many merchants of the town are worth, and therefore far exceed my credit, sir,” the merchant said.

"Go tell them that the Jew of Malta sent you, man," Barabas said. "Bah, who among them does not know who Barabas is?"

"I go now," the merchant said.

Barabas said to himself, "So, then, there's some of my ships arrived safely."

He then asked the merchant, who was starting to leave, "Sirrah, which of my ships are you the master of?"

The word "sirrah" was used to refer to a man of lower social status than the speaker.

The merchant replied, "I am the master of the *Speranza*, sir."

In Italian, "*speranza*" means hope.

"And didn't you see my fleet of merchant ships at Alexandria?" Barabas said. "You could not come from Egypt or by Cairo, but at the entry there into the sea, where the Nile River pays his tribute by flowing into the Mediterranean Sea. You necessarily must sail by Alexandria."

"I neither saw them nor inquired about them," the merchant said. "But this we heard some of our seamen say: They wondered how you dared to trust such crazed and unseaworthy vessels with so much wealth, and during so far a journey."

Barabas said sarcastically, "Tush, they are wise!"

He added without sarcasm, "I know my ships and their strength. But go, go on your way, unload your ship, and tell my commercial agent to bring his bill of lading in."

The merchant exited.

Barabas said to himself, "And yet I wonder about this fleet of merchant ships."

A second merchant arrived and said, "Know, Barabas, that your fleet of merchant ships from Alexandria rides in Malta roadstead, aka harbor, laden with riches, and an extremely great store of Persian silks, of gold, and of lustrous orient pearl."

"How does it happen that you didn't come with those other ships that sailed by Egypt?" Barabas asked.

"Sir, we didn't see them," the second merchant said.

"Perhaps they coasted round by the shore of Crete to take on a load of olive oil or they had some other business to do," Barabas said. "But it was ill done by you to come so far without the aid and protective escort of their ships."

Pirates infested the Mediterranean, and merchant ships needed protection.

"Sir, we were escorted by a Spanish fleet that never left us until we were within a league — three miles — of Malta," the second merchant said. "The Spanish fleet was pursuing the galleys of the Turks."

"Oh, they were going up to Sicily in pursuit of the Turks," Barabas said. "Well, go and tell the merchants and my men to dispatch the customs business and come ashore and see the freight unloaded."

"I go now," the second merchant said, exiting.

Barabas said to himself, "Thus rolls and flows our fortune in by land and sea, and thus are we on every side enriched. These are the blessings promised to the Jews, and herein was old Abram's happiness."

Genesis 15:18 states, "*In that same day the Lord made a covenant with Abram, saying, Unto thy seed have I given this land: from the river of Egypt unto the great river Euphrates*" (1599 Geneva Bible).

Exodus 3:17 states, "*Therefore I did say, I will bring you out of the affliction of Egypt unto the land of the Canaanites, and the Hittites, and the Amorites, and the Perizzites, and the Hivites, and the Jebusites, unto a land that floweth with milk and honey*" (1599 Geneva Bible).

Barabas continued, "What more may heaven do for earthly men than thus to pour out plenty in their laps, ripping the bowels of the earth for them, making the seas their servant, and making the winds drive their richly laden merchant ships with propitious blasts of wind? Who hates me but for my happiness, good fortune, and prosperity? Or who is honored now but for his wealth?

"Rather had I, a Jew, be hated thus, than be pitied in a Christian poverty. For I can see no fruits in all their faith except malice, falsehood, and excessive pride, which I think doesn't fit their profession of faith."

Matthew 7:18-20 (1599 Geneva Bible) states this:

18 A good tree cannot bring forth evil fruit, neither can a corrupt tree bring forth good fruit.

19 Every tree that bringeth not forth good fruit, is hewn down, and cast into the fire.

20 Therefore by their fruits ye shall know them.

Barabas continued, "Perhaps some hapless, unfortunate man has a conscience, and for his conscience he lives in beggary.

"They say we Jews are a scattered nation."

Deuteronomy 28:25 states, "*And the Lord shall cause thee to fall before thine enemies: thou shalt come out one way against them, and shalt flee seven ways before them, and shalt be scattered through all the kingdoms of the earth*" (1599 Geneva Bible).

Barabas continued, "I cannot tell, but we have scrambled and gathered up more wealth by far than those who brag of faith.

"There's Kirriah Jairim, the great Jew of Greece; Obed in Bairseth, Nones in Portugal, myself in Malta, some in Italy, many in France, and wealthy every one — yes, wealthier by far than any Christian.

"I must confess that we don't become kings. That's not our fault. Alas, our numbers are few, and crowns either come by succession or are gained by force, and often I have heard told that nothing violent can be permanent.

"Give us a peaceful rule; make kings of Christians, who thirst so much for sovereignty.

"I have no load of trouble, nor many children — only one sole daughter, whom I hold as dear as Agamemnon did his Iphigenia, and all I have is hers."

Agamemnon was the leader of the Greeks against the Trojans during the Trojan War. The goddess Artemis forced him to sacrifice Iphigenia in order to get favorable winds to blow the Greek ships to Troy.

Barabas looked up and asked, "But who comes here?"

Three Jews arrived.

The first Jew said to the other, "Tush, don't say that — it was done because of cunning political policy."

"Come, therefore, let us go to Barabas," the second Jew said, "for he can counsel best in these affairs — and here he comes."

Barabas walked over to greet them, saying, "Why, how are you now, countrymen? Why do you flock like this to me in multitudes?"

The three Jews represented all the Jews of Malta.

Barabas continued, "What accident's happening to the Jews?"

"A fleet of warlike galleys, Barabas, have come from Turkey and lie in our harbor," the first Jew said, "and the rulers of Malta sit in the council house this day to receive them and their ambassador and his retinue."

"Why, let them come, as long as they don't come to make war," Barabas said, "or let them make war, as long as we are conquerors."

He thought, *Indeed, let them combat, conquer, and kill all, as long as they spare me, my daughter, and my wealth.*

"If they came here for confirmation of an alliance, they would not have come in such a warlike manner as this," the first Jew said.

"I fear their coming will afflict us all," the second Jew said.

"Foolish men, why do you dream of their multitudes?" Barabas said. "What need do they have to negotiate peace with those with whom they already have a peace treaty? The Turks and those of Malta are in league. Tut, tut, there is some other matter going on."

"Why, Barabas, they come either for peace or for war," the first Jew said.

"Perhaps for neither," Barabas said, "but to pass along Malta and head towards Venice by the Adriatic Sea. They have attacked the Venetians many times, but they never could reach their military goal."

"And that is very wisely said," the third Jew said. "It may be so."

"But there's a meeting in the Senate House," the second Jew said, "and all the Jews in Malta must be there."

"Hmm, all the Jews in Malta must be there?" Barabas said. "Yes, likely enough. Why, then let every man prepare himself and be there for fashion's sake — as a matter of form. If anything shall there concern our welfare, assure yourselves I'll look —"

He stopped and thought, *I'll look after me and my affairs.*

The first Jew interrupted, "I know you will."

He then said, "Well, brethren, let us go."

"Let's take our leaves," the second Jew said.

Barabas said to the second Jew, "Do so."

"Farewell, good Barabas," the second Jew said.

Barabas said, "Farewell, Zaareth; farewell, Temainte."

The three Jews exited.

Barabas said to himself, "And, Barabas, now search this secret out. Summon your senses; call your wits together: These foolish men mistake the matter completely. Malta did contribute for a long time to the Turkish Emperor."

True, but Malta was behind on the tribute: It had not paid the tribute for the past ten years.

Barabas continued, "This tribute — all in cunning political policy, I fear — the Turks have let increase to such a sum that all the wealth of Malta cannot pay it. And now by that advantage the Turkish Emperor thinks, probably, to seize upon the town — yes, that is what he seeks.

"However the world goes, I'll make things sure for Number One, and seek in time to anticipate, intercept, and prevent the worst, warily guarding that which I have got. *Ego mihimet sum semper proximus.*"

The Latin means, "I am always nearest to myself"; in other words, "I always look out for Number One." It is adapted from a line in Terence's *Andria*, "*Proximus sum egomet mihi*" (IV.i.12).

Barabas said, "Why, let them enter — let them take the town."

Ferneze, the Governor of Malta; the Knights of Malta; Selim Calymath, a son of the Turkish Emperor; and some Pashas of the Turkish Emperor met together. Pashas are Turkish aristocrats and military leaders. Some Maltese officers were also present.

Governor Ferneze of Malta said, "Now, Pashas, what do you demand from us?"

"Know, Knights of Malta, that we came from Rhodes, from Cyprus, Crete, and those other isles that lie among the Mediterranean seas," Callapine said.

The Mediterranean seas are the Adriatic, Aegean, Euxine, Terrene, etc.

"What's Cyprus, Crete, and those other isles to us or Malta?" Governor Ferneze of Malta asked. "What do you want from us?"

"The ten years of tribute that remains unpaid," Callapine said.

"Alas, my lord, the sum is excessive!" Governor Ferneze of Malta said. "I hope your highness will be considerate toward us."

"I wish, grave and worthy-of-respect Governor, it were in my power to favor you," Selim Calymath said, "but it is my father's cause, wherein I may not, nay, I dare not dally."

"Then give us leave to talk privately, great Selim Calymath," Governor Ferneze of Malta said.

"Everyone, stand to the side, and let the Knights of Malta determine what they will do," Selim Calymath said.

The Turks moved to the side, and Governor Ferneze of Malta began to consult quietly with his advisors.

Selim Calymath continued, "And send word to keep our galleys under sail, for happily — if all goes well — we shall not tarry here."

He then said, "Now, Governor, what have you decided?"

Governor Ferneze of Malta said, "We have decided this: Since your hard conditions are such that you must have the ten years of tribute that is past due, we ask that we may have time to make a collection from among the inhabitants of Malta fort."

"That's more than we are authorized to do in our commission," Callapine said.

"Callapine, show a little courtesy!" Selim Calymath said. "Let's learn the amount of time they require to collect the tribute money; perhaps it is not long. And it is more kingly to obtain by peace than to enforce conditions by constraint."

A proverb states, "It is better to obtain by love than force."

Selim Calymath asked, "What respite are you asking for, Governor Ferneze?"

"Only a month," he replied.

"We grant you a delay of a month, but see that you keep your promise," Callapine said. "Now we will launch our galleys back again to sea, where we'll wait during the respite you have taken, and then send our messenger for the money.

"Farewell, Great Governor, and brave Knights of Malta."

"And may all good fortune wait on Selim Calymath," Governor Ferneze said.

The Turks exited.

"Go, one of you, and call those Jews of Malta here," Governor Ferneze said. "Weren't they summoned to appear today?"

"They were, my lord," the officer said, "and here they come."

Barabas and the three Jews arrived.

"Have you determined what to say to them?" the first Knight of Malta asked.

"Yes," Governor Ferneze said. "Give me time to act."

He then said, "Hebrews, now come near. Great Selim Calymath, who is the son of the Emperor of Turkey, has arrived to collect from us ten years of tribute that is past due. Now, then, here know that it concerns us."

"Then, my good lord, to keep your quiet, peaceful state of affairs still, your lordship shall do well to let them have it," Barabas said.

"Be quiet, Barabas, there's more to it than that," Governor Ferneze said. "We have calculated to what this ten years' tribute will amount, but we cannot raise that amount of money because of the wars that have robbed our store of money and therefore we request your aid."

Barabas deliberately misunderstood what Governor Ferneze had said. He pretended instead to believe that Governor Ferneze had asked the Jews to serve as soldiers.

"Alas, my lord, we are no soldiers," Barabas said. "And what would our aid amount to against so great a prince?"

"Tut, Jew, we know thou are no soldier," the first Knight of Malta said. "Thou are a merchant and a moneyed man, and it is thy money, Barabas, that we seek."

In this society, "you" was a respectful form of address. People of high status used words such as "thou" and "thy" and "thine" to refer to a person of lower status.

"What, my lord? My money?" Barabas asked.

"Thine money and the money of the rest of the Jews, for, to be short, among you it must be obtained," Governor Ferneze said.

"Alas, my lord, most of us are poor," the first Jew said.

"Then let the rich give more," Governor Ferneze said.

"Are foreigners to be taxed with your tribute?" Barabas asked.

The Maltese regarded the Jews as foreigners and not as true citizens of Malta.

"Have foreigners our permission to get their wealth?" the second Knight of Malta said. "Then let them with us contribute."

"How?" Barabas said. "Equally?"

"No, Jew," Governor Ferneze said, "Like infidels. For through our tolerance of your hateful lives, who stand accursed in the sight of heaven, these taxes and afflictions have befallen."

Many Christians of the time believed that the Jews were responsible for the crucifixion of Jesus Christ. Governor Ferneze was saying that because Malta had allowed the Jews to live there, God was punishing Malta.

He continued, "And therefore this is what we have determined to do —"

He ordered an officer, "Read there the articles of our decrees."

The officer read out loud, *"First, the tribute money of the Turks shall all be levied among the Jews, and each of them to pay one half of his estate."*

"What! Half his estate!" Barabas said.

He thought, *I hope don't you mean mine.*

"Read on," Governor Ferneze ordered.

The officer read out loud, *"Secondly, he who refuses to pay shall immediately become a Christian."*

"What! A Christian!" Barabas said.

He then thought, *Hmm, what shall I do here?*

The officer read out loud, "*Lastly, he who refuses to do this shall absolutely lose all he has.*"

"Oh, my lord, we will give half of what we have," the three Jews said.

Barabas said to the three Jews, "Oh, earth-mettled — dull-witted — villains, you are no Hebrews born! Will you basely thus submit yourselves and leave your goods under their control?"

"Why, Barabas, will thou be christened?" Governor Ferneze asked.

"No, Governor, I will be no convert," Barabas said.

"Then pay thy half," Governor Ferneze said.

"Why, do you know what you did by this trick?" Barabas said. "Half of my possessions is a city's wealth. Governor, it was not gotten so easily, nor will I part so easily with it."

"Sir, half is the fine of our decree," Governor Ferneze said. "Either pay that, or we will seize all of your wealth."

"*Corpo di Dio!*" Barabas said.

The Italian means, "By God's body!"

Governor Ferneze made a sign to the officers, who exited.

Barabas said, "Wait! You shall have half of my wealth. Let me be treated just as my brethren are."

"No, Jew, thou have denied the articles, and now your denial cannot be recalled," Governor Ferneze said.

"Will you then steal my goods?" Barabas asked. "Is theft the ground and basis of your religion?"

"No, Jew," Governor Ferneze said. "We take in particular thine wealth to save the ruin of a multitude, and it is better that one go without for a common good than that many shall perish for an individual man."

John 11:50 states, "*Nor yet do you consider that it is expedient for us, that one man die for the people, and that the whole nation perish not*" (1599 Geneva Bible).

Governor Ferneze continued, "Yet, Barabas, we will not banish thee, but here in Malta, where thou got thy wealth, continue to live, and if thou can, get more wealth."

"Christians, what or how can I multiply?" Barabas said. "Of nought is nothing made."

Christians believed that God created the universe *ex nihilo* — out of nothing.

"From nought at first thou came to little wealth," the first Knight of Malta said. "From little thou came to more, from more to most. If your first curse falls heavy on thy head, and makes thee poor and scorned of all the world, it is not our fault, but the fault of thy inherent sin."

The "first curse" occurred when the Jews demanded the crucifixion of Christ. Matthew 27:25 states, "*Then answered all the people, and said, His blood be on us, and on our children*" (1599 Geneva Bible).

Some Christians at this time believed that this curse placed on Jews was hereditary.

"What! Do you bring scripture to confirm your wrongs?" Barabas asked.

A proverb stated, "The Devil can cite scripture for his purpose."

He continued, "Preach me not out of my possessions. Some Jews are wicked" — he thought, *as all Christians are* — "but say that the tribe that I descended from were all in general cast away and rejected and damned by God for sin, shall I be tried for their transgression? The man who deals righteously shall live."

Proverbs 10:2 states, "*The treasures of wickedness profit nothing: but righteousness delivereth from death*" (1599 Geneva Bible).

Proverbs 10:16 states, "*The labor of the righteous tendeth to life: but the revenues of the wicked to sin*" (1599 Geneva Bible).

Proverbs 12:28 states, "*Life is in the way of righteousness, and in that pathway there is no death*" (1599 Geneva Bible).

Barabas added, "And which of you can charge me otherwise?"

John 8:46 states, "*Which of you can rebuke me of sin? and if I say the truth, why do ye not believe me?*" (1599 Geneva Bible).

"Bah, wretched Barabas!" Governor Ferneze said. "Aren't thou ashamed to justify thyself like this, as if we didn't know thy profession?"

The word "profession" means 1) "religious creed," and 2) "occupation."

Governor Ferneze continued, "If thou rely upon thy righteousness, be patient, and thy riches will increase. Excess of wealth is the cause of covetousness, and covetousness — oh, it is a monstrous sin."

"Yes, but theft is worse," Barabas said. "Tush, don't take wealth from me then, for that is theft, and if you rob me like that, I must be forced to steal and gather more."

"Grave Governor, don't listen to his exclamations," the first Knight of Malta said. "Convert his mansion to a nunnery. His house will harbor many holy nuns."

"It shall be done," Governor Ferneze said.

The officers returned.

"Now, officers, have you finished?" Governor Ferneze asked.

"Yes, my lord," the first officer said. "We have seized the goods and wares of Barabas, which, being valued, amount to more than all the wealth in Malta. And from the other Jews we have seized half their wealth. Then we'll take order for the residue."

He meant that now they would start converting the property they had seized to cash so they could pay the tribute to the Turks. The "residue" was what remained to be done of their orders.

"Well, then, my lord, tell me, are you satisfied?" Barabas asked. "You have my goods, my money, and my wealth, my ships, my store of possessions, and all that I enjoyed. And, having all, you can request no more, unless your unrelenting flinty hearts suppress all pity in your stony breasts, and now shall move you to take my life."

"No, Barabas," Governor Ferneze said. "To stain our hands with blood is far from us and our profession."

"Why, I esteem the injury far less to take the lives of miserable men than be the causers of their misery," Barabas said. "You have my wealth, the labor of my life, the comfort of my old age, and my children's hope."

Barabas had only one child: a daughter. He had said "children's hope" in an attempt to arouse pity.

He added, "And therefore never make distinctions about the wrong — don't try to minimize the wrong you have done to me by saying you won't kill me."

Barabas would agree with Machiavelli's observation that "above all things [the prince] must keep his hands off the property of others, because men more quickly forget the death of their father than the loss of their patrimony."

"Be content, Barabas," Governor Ferneze said. "Thou has received nought ... but right and justice."

In this culture, "nought" could mean "nothing," 2) "poverty," or 3) "evil."

"Your extreme right does me exceeding wrong," Barabas said.

Cicero wrote "*summum ius, summa iniuria*" in *De Officiis* I.x.33. Walter Miller translated this as "More law, less justice." In other words, the more strictly justice is enforced, the more injustice it creates.

Barabas continued, "But take it to you, in the devil's name!"

"Come, let us go in and gather from the sale of these goods the money for this tribute of the Turkish Emperor," Governor Ferneze said.

"It is necessary that that is looked to," the first Knight of Malta said, "for if we miss our deadline, we break the treaty, and that will prove to be only a foolish policy."

Governor Ferneze and the Knights of Malta exited, leaving behind Barabas and the three other Jews.

"Aye, policy?" Barabas said. "That's their profession, and not simplicity, as they suggest."

"Policy" meant "devious and cunning Machiavellian political policy," or in other words, "cunning trickery," while "simplicity" meant "honesty and straightforwardness."

Barabas was pointing out the hypocrisy of the Maltese Christians. They were practicing Machiavellian politics, not Christian simplicity and virtue.

2 Corinthians 11:3 states, "*But I fear lest as the serpent beguiled Eve through his subtlety, so your minds should be corrupt from the simplicity that is in Christ*" (1599 Geneva Bible).

Barabas knelt and swore a curse: "Inflict upon them the plagues of Egypt and the curse of heaven, the earth's barrenness, and all men's hatred, thou great Primus Motor! And here upon my knees, striking the earth, I condemn their souls to everlasting pains, and extreme tortures of the fiery deep. I curse those who thus have dealt with me in my distress."

The Primus Motor comes from Aristotelian thought — the Primus Motor is the first cause of motion in the universe. Some Christians sometimes use the term "Prime Mover" to refer to God.

Barabas stood up.

"Oh, yet be patient, gentle Barabas," the first Jew said.

"Oh, foolish brethren, who were born to see this day of my unhappiness," Barabas said, "why do you stand thus unmoved with my laments? Why don't you weep to think upon my wrongs? Why don't I pine and die in this distress?"

"Why, Barabas, just as hard as you take your misfortune do we endure the cruel handling of ourselves in this affair," the first Jew said. "Thou see they have taken half our goods."

"Why did you yield to their extortion?" Barabas asked. "You were a multitude, and I was only one, and from only me have they taken all."

"Yet, brother Barabas, remember Job," the first Jew said.

In the Biblical Book of Job, Job is a good man whose prosperity, children, and health are taken away from him when God gives Satan permission to do these things. Job struggles with the Problem of Evil and asks God to explain His actions.

This is the Problem of Evil:

Premise 1: If God is omnipotent (all-powerful), then he could prevent evil.

Premise 2: If God is omnibenevolent (all-good), then he would prevent evil.

Premise 3: Evil exists.

Conclusion: Either God is not omnipotent, or God is not omnibenevolent.

"Why do you tell me about Job?" Barabas said. "I know that his wealth was written thus: He had seven thousand sheep, three thousand camels, and two hundred yoke of laboring oxen, and five hundred she-asses. But for every one of those, had they been valued impartially at a fair price, I had at home, and in my fleet of merchant ships and other ships that came from Egypt most recently, as much as would have bought his beasts and him, and yet have kept enough to live upon. So then not he, but I, may curse the day, thy fatal birthday, forlorn Barabas, that clouds of darkness may enclose my flesh, and hide these extreme sorrows from my eyes, for I have toiled to inherit here only the months of vain striving and loss of time, and painful nights have been appointed me."

"Good Barabas, be patient," the second Jew said.

"Aye, I ask you to please leave me in my patience — my stoic suffering," Barabas said. "You who were never possessed of wealth are content without it. But give him liberty at least to mourn, he who in a field amid his enemies sees his soldiers slain, himself disarmed, and knows no way of gaining his recovery.

Aye, let me sorrow for this sudden misfortune. It is in the trouble of my spirit that I speak. Great injuries are not so soon forgotten."

"Come, let us leave him," the first Jew said. "In his angry mood, our words will but increase his frenzy."

"Let's go, then," the second Jew said. "But, trust me, it is a misery to see a man in such affliction."

He then said, "Farewell, Barabas."

"Aye, may you fare well," Barabas said.

The three Jews exited.

Barabas said, "See the simplicity of these base slaves, who, because the villains have no intelligence themselves, think that I am a senseless lump of clay that will with every water wash to dirt."

The image meant that the Jews regarded Barabas as a person who would fall to pieces at every crisis.

He continued, "No, Barabas is born to better fortune and framed of finer materials than common men who measure nought but by the present time. A person with far-reaching thought will exercise his deepest intelligence and cunningly plan and provide for the time to come, for evils are apt to happen every day."

Seeing his daughter coming toward him, he asked himself, "But whither wends my beauteous Abigail?"

Abigail, Barabas' daughter, walked over to him.

Barabas asked, "Oh, what has made my lovely daughter sad? What, woman! Don't moan over a little loss. Thy father has enough in store for thee."

She replied, "Not for myself, but aged Barabas, father, for thee laments Abigail. But I will learn to leave these fruitless tears, and, incited thereto by my afflictions, I will run to the Senate House with fierce protests, and in the Senate I will reprehend them all and rend their hearts by tearing my hair until they redress the wrongs done to my father."

"No, Abigail," Barabas said. "Things past recovery are hardly cured with exclamations."

A proverb stated, "Past care, past cure."

He continued, "Be silent, daughter. Patient endurance breeds ease, and time, which in this sudden crisis cannot help us, may in the future yield us an opportunity.

"Besides, my girl, think me not all so foolish as negligently to lose so much without making provision for thyself and me. Fearing the worst of this before it fell, I secretly hid ten thousand Portuguese gold coins, besides great pearls, rich costly jewels, and an infinite number of precious stones."

"Where, father?" Abigail asked.

"In my house, my girl," Barabas replied.

"Then they shall never be seen by Barabas," Abigail said, "for the Maltese officials have seized thy house and wares."

"But they will give me permission once more, I trust, to go into my house," Barabas said.

"That they may not," Abigail said, "for there I left the Governor placing nuns, displacing me, and of thy house the nuns intend to make a nunnery, where none but their own religious sect and sex must enter in; men are completely barred."

"My gold, my gold, and all my wealth is gone," Barabas said. "You unfair heavens, have I deserved this plague? What! Will you thus oppose me, unlucky and malignant stars, to make me desperate in my poverty? And knowing me impatient in distress, do you think that I am so mad that I will hang myself so that I may vanish over the earth into air and leave no memory that I ever existed?

"No, I will live, nor will I loathe this my life. And since you leave me in the ocean thus to sink or swim, and to live by my wits and fend for myself, I'll rouse my senses, and awaken myself.

"Daughter, I have it. Thou perceive the plight wherein these Christians have oppressed me. Be guided by me, for in extremity we ought to bar no policy. We must make use of any means, plan, and strategy that will help us."

Abigail replied, "Father, whatever it is that will injure them who have so manifestly wronged us, what won't Abigail do?"

"Why, good," Barabas said. "Then thus: Did thou tell me that they have turned my house into a nunnery, and some nuns are there?"

"I did."

"Then, Abigail, there must my girl entreat the abbess to be admitted."

"How, as a nun?" Abigail asked.

"Yes, daughter, for religion hides many acts of evil-doing from suspicion," Barabas said.

"Yes, but father, they will suspect me there."

"Let them suspect, but thou shall be so precise and strict in religious matters that they may think your entreaty is done from holiness," Barabas said. "Entreat them courteously, and give them friendly speech, and seem to them as if thy sins were great, until thou have gotten admitted to the nunnery."

"If I profess that, father, I shall greatly lie," Abigail said.

She meant 1) profess that she had converted to Christianity, and 2) profess that her sins were great. Barabas understood her to mean #1 only.

"Bah!" Barabas said. "It is as good to lie about a conversion you don't mean as to at first tell the truth about being a Christian and then act in such a way as to make that truth a lie."

He paused and then added, "A counterfeit profession is better than hidden, undetected hypocrisy."

"Well, father, let's say I am admitted into the nunnery, what then shall follow?" Abigail asked.

"This shall then follow: In my house — the nunnery — I have hidden, concealed underneath the plank that runs along the upper chamber floor, the gold and jewels that I kept for thee."

Seeing two friars, the Abbess, and a nun coming, he said, "But here they come. Be cunning, Abigail."

"Then, father, go with me."

"No, Abigail, in this it is necessary that I not be seen," Barabas said, "for I will pretend to be offended with thee for seeming to have converted to Christianity. Keep your true self hidden, my girl, for this must fetch my gold."

Barabas hid himself as the friars Jacomo and Barnardine arrived with the Abbess and a nun.

"Sisters, we now are almost at the new-made nunnery," Friar Jacomo said.

"All the better," the Abbess said, "for we love not to be seen. It has been thirty winters since some of us did stray so far among the multitude."

"But, madam, this house and the sources of water of this new-made nunnery will much delight you," Friar Jacomo said.

Barabas' property may have included a well and a pond.

"It may be so," the Abbess said. "But who comes here?"

Abigail said, "Grave Abbess, and you happy virgins' guides, pity the state of a distressed maiden."

"Who are thou, daughter?" the Abbess asked.

"The hopeless, despairing daughter of a hapless, unfortunate Jew — the Jew of Malta, wretched Barabas — formerly the owner of a splendid house, which they have now turned to a nunnery."

"Well, daughter, tell us, what is thy suit with us?" the Abbess asked. "What do you want?"

"Fearing the afflictions that my father feels proceed from sin or lack of faith in us Jews, I want to pass away my life in penitence and be a novice in your nunnery in order to make atonement for my troubled soul," Abigail said.

"There is no doubt, brother, that this proceeds from the spirit," Friar Jacomo said. "This proceeds from divine influence."

John 3:5-6 (1599 Geneva Bible) states this:

5 Jesus answered, Verily, verily I say unto thee, except that a man be born of water and of the Spirit, he cannot enter into the kingdom of God.

6 That which is born of the flesh, is flesh: and that that is born of the Spirit, is spirit.

Friar Barnardine replied, "Yes, and of a moving spirit, too, brother."

A "moving spirit" is one that excites the passions. The spirit that could be moved is Abigail's, spiritually, or Barnardine's, sexually.

The word "spirit" can mean "soul," 2) "Holy Spirit, aka Holy Ghost," and 3) "semen (vital spirits)."

He added, "But come, let us entreat that she may be entertained."

The word "entertained" can mean 1) "admitted (into the nunnery)," and 2) "seduced."

The Abbess said to Abigail, "Well, daughter, we admit you for a nun."

"First let me as a novice learn to shape my solitary life to your strict laws, and let me lodge where I was accustomed to lie," Abigail said.

A novice has not yet taken the vows of a nun, but is serving a time of probation to see whether she ought to take those vows. Abigail was worried about committing sin by breaking the vows of a nun.

She continued, "I do not doubt, by your divine precepts and my own industry, but to profit much."

Listening, Barabas said to himself, "As much profit, I hope, as all I hid is worth."

"Come, daughter, follow us," the Abbess said.

Coming out of hiding, Barabas said, "Why, what is this? Abigail, what are thou doing among these hateful Christians?"

"Don't hinder her, thou man of little faith," Friar Jacomo said, "for she has mortified herself — she has become dead to worldly things."

"What!" Barabas said. "Mortified!"

"And she has been admitted to the sisterhood," Friar Jacomo added.

"Child of perdition — child of sin and damnation — and thy father's shame, what will thou do among these hateful fiends?" Barabas asked Abigail. "I command thee on my blessing that thou leave these devils and their damned heresy."

Abigail moved toward him and said, "Father, give me —"

She had started to ask her father for his blessing.

"No, stay back, Abigail," Barabas said loudly.

He whispered to her, "And think upon the jewels and the gold. The board under which they are hidden is marked thus" — he made a sign of an obelus that looked like a dagger although a Christian would say it looked like a cross.

He said out loud, "Stay away, accursed daughter, from thy father's sight!"

"Barabas, although thou are in misbelief and do not think correctly about God and will not see thine own afflictions, yet let thy daughter be no longer spiritually blind," Friar Jacomo said.

"Blind, friar?" Barabas said. "I am unmoved by thy persuasions and beliefs."

He whispered to Abigail, who had stayed near him, "The board is marked thus" — he again made a sign of an obelus. "That sign marks the board that covers the treasure."

He said out loud to Friar Jacomo, "For I had rather die than see her thus — a Christian."

He then asked Abigail out loud, "Will thou forsake me, too, in my distress, seduced daughter?"

He was saying that Christianity had seduced Abigail.

He then whispered to her, "Go, and don't forget what I have told you."

He said out loud, "Does it become Jews to be so credulous? Is it fitting that Jews can be so easily persuaded by Christian arguments?"

He whispered to Abigail, "Tomorrow early I'll be at the door."

He said out loud to her, "No, don't come near me. If thou will be damned, forget me, don't see me; and so, be gone."

He whispered to her, "Farewell; remember tomorrow morning."

He said out loud to her, "Out, out, thou wretch! Get out of my sight!"

Barabas exited, and then the others exited in another direction.

Before they exited, Mathias had arrived and saw and heard some of their conversation.

He said to himself, "Who's this? Fair Abigail, the rich Jew's daughter, become a nun? Her father's sudden fall has humbled her, and brought her down to this.

"Tut, she were fitter for a tale of love than to be tired out with prayers, and better would she far become a bed, embraced in a friendly lover's arms, than rise at midnight to attend a solemn, ceremonious mass."

Lodowick, the son of Governor Ferneze, arrived. Lodowick and Mathias were friends.

"Why, how are you now, Don Mathias?" Lodowick asked. "Down in the dumps?"

"Believe me, noble Lodowick, I have seen the strangest sight, in my opinion, that ever I beheld," Mathias said.

"What was it, I ask you?"

"A fair young maiden, scarcely fourteen years of age, and the sweetest flower in Cytherea's field."

Venus was sometimes called Cytherea because she was born in the sea near the island of Cythera.

Mathias continued, "She has been cropped from the pleasures of the fruitful earth and strangely metamorphosed into a nun."

"But tell me, who was she?" Lodowick asked.

"Why, the rich Jew's daughter."

"What! Barabas, whose goods were recently seized? Is she so fair?"

"And matchlessly beautiful," Mathias said. "If you had seen her, it would have moved your heart even if it were countermured — defensively fortified with two walls of brass — to love her, or at the least, to pity her."

"And if she is so fair as you report, it would be time well spent to go and visit her," Lodowick said. "What do you say? Shall we?"

"I must and will, sir," Mathias said. "There's no alternative."

"And so will I, too, or it shall go hard," Lodowick said.

"It shall go hard" could mean 1) "there will be trouble," 2) "it will happen unless opposed by overwhelming circumstances," and 3) "I will get an erection." Presumably, he would get an erection simply by thinking about her.

He said, "Farewell, Mathias."

Mathias replied, "Farewell, Lodowick."

CHAPTER 2

— 2.1 —

Unable to sleep, Barabas arrived at the nunnery — his old house — carrying a light in the darkness.

Talking to himself, he made a reference to the superstition that ravens were ill omens and would announce with their cries the coming death of a person: "Thus, like the sad presaging, foreboding raven that tolls the funeral bell for the sick man's passport to the Land of the Dead in her hollow beak, and in the shadow of the silent night shakes contagion from her sable wings, vexed and tormented runs poor Barabas with fatal curses towards these Christians."

He then said, "The uncertain pleasures of swift-footed time have taken their flight, and left me in despair, and of my former riches no more than bare remembrance remains, like the scar of a soldier who has no further comfort for his maim."

A maim is a serious, disabling wound such as one that results in amputation. Often, soldiers were not well compensated for suffering such wounds.

Barabas continued, "Oh, God, Thou Who with a fiery pillar by night led the sons of Israel through the dismal shades and out of Egypt, light the way for Abraham's offspring; and direct the hand of Abigail this night, or let the day turn to eternal darkness after this."

Exodus 13:21-22 (1599 Geneva Bible) states this:

21 And the Lord went before them by day in a pillar of a cloud to lead them the way, and by night in a pillar of fire to give them light, that they might go both by day and by night.

22 He took not away the pillar of the cloud by day, nor the pillar of fire by night from before the people.

Barabas continued, "No sleep can fasten on my watching, wakeful eyes, nor can quiet enter my agitated thoughts, until I have information from my Abigail."

Abigail appeared at a window on the second story of the new-made nunnery.

She said to herself, "Now I have fortunately found a time to search under the plank my father did designate."

She lifted the plank and said, "And here, behold, unseen, where I have found the gold, pearls, and jewels that he hid."

Not seeing Abigail, Barabas sat and said, "Now I remember those old women's words, who, in my days of wealth, would tell me winter's tales — tales suitable for passing long winter hours — and speak of spirits and ghosts that glide by night about the place where treasure has been hid, and now I think that I am one of those spirits and ghosts, for while I live, here lives my soul's sole hope, and when I die, here shall my spirit walk."

Not seeing Barabas, Abigail said, "Now if only my father's fortune were so good as to be here in this happy place! His fortune is not so happy. Yet when we parted last, he said he would see me in the morning. So then, gentle sleep, wherever his body rests, give charge to Morpheus, god of sleep and dreams, that he may dream a golden dream, and all of a sudden wake up, come, and receive the treasure I have found."

In Spanish, Barabas said, "*Bueno para todos mi ganado no era.*"

This means, "My gain is not good for everybody." In other words, he did not want everyone to take his wealth; instead, he wanted to keep it.

He continued, "It is as good to go on as to sit so sadly like this."

He stood up, saw a candle that Abigail had lit, and said, "But wait! What star shines yonder in the east? It is the loadstar — guiding light — of my life. It is Abigail."

He called, "Who's there?"

"Who's that calling?" Abigail asked.

"Be at peace, Abigail," Barabas said. "It is I."

"Then, father, here receive thy happiness," Abigail said.

"Do you have it?" Barabas asked.

"Here," she said, throwing down a bag of treasure. "Do you have it?"

As she threw down the other bags of treasure, she said, "There's more ... and more ... and more."

"Oh, my girl, my gold, my fortune, my felicity, strength to my soul, death to my enemy," Barabas said.

He said to his bags of treasure, "Welcome, the first beginner of my bliss."

He then said, "Oh, Abigail, Abigail, if only I had thee here, too, then my desires would be fully satisfied. But I will devise a way to get thee thy freedom from the nunnery.

"Oh, girl! Oh, gold! Oh, beauty! Oh, my bliss!"

He hugged his bags of treasure.

"Father, it draws close to midnight now," Abigail said, "and about this time the nuns begin to wake in order to sing the matins. To shun and avoid suspicion, therefore, let us part."

"Farewell, my joy, and by my fingers take a kiss from him who sends it from his soul," Barabas said, blowing her a kiss.

He then said, "Now, Phoebus Apollo, open the eyelids of the day, and in place of the raven wake the morning lark, so that I may hover with her in the air, singing over these moneybags, as she does over her young, '*Hermoso placer de los dineros.*'"

The Spanish words mean "the beautiful pleasure of money."

Governor Ferneze, the Knights of Malta, and some Maltese officers met together. With them was the newly arrived Spanish Vice-Admiral del Bosco, who had not yet identified himself.

"Now, Captain, tell us to where thou are bound, from where comes thy ship that anchors in our harbor, and why thou came ashore without our leave?" Governor Ferneze asked Martin del Bosco.

He replied, "Governor of Malta, to here I am bound. My ship, the *Flying Dragon*, is from Spain, and so am I. Martin del Bosco is my name, and I am Vice-Admiral to the Catholic King — the King of Spain."

"It is true, my lord," the first Knight of Malta said. "Therefore, treat him well."

Vice-Admiral Martin del Bosco said, "Our freight is slaves — Grecians, Turks, and African Moors. Recently upon the coast of Corsica, because we declined to lower our sails in respect to the Turkish fleet, their creeping, slow-moving galleys chased us. Because of lack of wind, they had the advantage over us at first, but suddenly the wind began to rise, and then we luffed and tacked — turned and sailed zigzag into the wind to face the Turkish fleet — and fought at our ease.

"Some Turkish ships we set on fire, and many Turkish ships we sank, but one ship among the rest became our prize. The Turkish Captains were slain; the rest remain our slaves, of whom we would make sale in Malta here."

The Spanish ship had not lowered its sails to show respect to the Turkish fleet, so the fleet had chased it. At first the slow-moving Turkish fleet more than kept up with the Spanish ship, but the wind grew stronger, and the Spanish ship, which with the wind was faster and more maneuverable than the Turkish fleet, turned and fought and defeated the Turkish fleet.

"Martin del Bosco, I have heard of thee," Governor Ferneze said. "Welcome to Malta, and to all of us. But to admit a sale of these thy Turks, we may not, nay, we dare not give consent, by reason of a tributary treaty that we have made with Turkey."

The tributary treaty was a peace treaty between Malta and Turkey, but it required the Maltese to pay tribute to the Turks.

"Martin Del Bosco, as thou love and honor us, persuade our Governor to act against the Turkish Emperor," the first Knight of Malta said. "This truce we have was made only because of the Turks' hope of gold, and with that sum the Turkish Emperor craves we would be able to wage war. We can use the tribute money to arm ourselves against the Turks."

The Maltese could do that especially if they had Spanish support.

"Will the Knights of Malta be in league with Turks," Vice-Admiral Martin del Bosco said, "and basely buy that peace, too, for sums of gold? My lord, remember that, to Europe's shame, the Christian isle of Rhodes, from whence you came, was recently lost, and you Knights were installed in office in Malta here to be at deadly enmity with Turks."

The Knights of Malta are the Knights of Saint John of Jerusalem. Previously, the Knights of Saint John of Jerusalem had their headquarters on the island of Rhodes, but in 1522, after a siege, the Turks conquered the island. In 1530, King Charles I of Spain, who was also the King of Sicily, allowed them to settle at Malta, where they established their headquarters.

"Captain, we know it," Governor Ferneze said, "but our force is small."

Vice-Admiral Martin del Bosco asked, "What is the sum that Calymath requires?"

"A hundred thousand crowns," Governor Ferneze answered.

"My lord and king has title to this isle, and he means quickly to expel the Turks from here," Vice-Admiral Martin del Bosco said. "Therefore, take my advice, and keep the gold.

"I'll write to his majesty the King of Spain for aid, and I will not depart until I see you free of compelled obligations to the Turkish Emperor."

"On this condition thy Turkish captives shall be sold," Governor Ferneze said. "Go, officers, and immediately put them on display in the marketplace."

The Maltese officers exited.

Governor Ferneze continued, "Bosco, thou shall be Malta's general. We and our warlike Knights will follow thee against these barbarous, misbelieving, pagan Turks."

"So shall you imitate those you succeed," Vice-Admiral Martin del Bosco said. "For when the Turks' hideous force surrounded the island of Rhodes, small though the number of Knights of Rhodes was who kept the town, they fought it out, and not a man survived to bring the hapless news to Christendom."

The important point was that the Knights of Rhodes fought the Turks, just as the Knights of Malta should and would.

Governor Ferneze said, "So will we fight it out. Come, let's go."

He then addressed Calymath, who was not actually present: "Proud daring Calymath, instead of gold we'll send thee bullets wrapped in smoke and fire. Claim tribute wherever thou will, we are resolved to resist you. Honor is bought with blood and not with gold."

Some Maltese officers arrived with the slaves.

"This is the marketplace," the first officer said. "Here let them stand. Don't be afraid that they won't sell, for they'll be quickly bought."

"Everyone's price is written on his back," the second officer said, "and so much they must yield, or not be sold."

Barabas arrived.

"Here comes the Jew," the first officer said. "If his goods had not been seized, he'd give us ready cash for all of the slaves."

Barabas said to himself, "In spite of these swine-eating Christians — an unchosen nation, never circumcised —"

The Jews were the chosen people — they were chosen to have a special relationship with God.

Psalm 33:12 states, *"Blessed is that nation, whose God is the Lord: even the people that he hath chosen for his inheritance"* (1599 Geneva Bible).

He continued, "— such as, poor villains, were never thought of until Titus and Vespasian conquered us —"

In 66 C.E., Vespasian, then the Roman commander in Palestine, put down a Jewish revolt against the Romans. In 69 C.E. Vespasian became Roman Emperor, and in 70 C.E. Titus, Vespasian's son, conquered Jerusalem.

He continued, "— I have become as wealthy as I was. They hoped my daughter would have been a nun; but she's at home, and I have bought a house as great and fair as is the Governor Ferneze's. And there, in spite of Malta, I will dwell, having Ferneze's hand, whose heart I'll have, aye, and his son's, too, or it shall go hard."

Governor Ferneze had allowed Barabas to prosper, giving him the assurance of a legal document in his own handwriting or perhaps a handshake, but Barabas wanted revenge against him and his heart — and only overpowering obstacles would prevent him from getting that revenge.

Barabas continued, "I am not of the priestly tribe of Levi, I. The priestly tribe of Levi can very soon forget an injury."

Joshua 21 names the towns the Levites were given to live in, including some cities that were refuges for people accused of murder.

Joshua 20:1-3 (1599 Geneva Bible) states this:

1 The Lord also spake unto Joshua, saying,

2 Speak to the children of Israel, and say, Appoint you cities of refuge, whereof I spake unto you by the hand of Moses,

3 That the slayer that killeth any person by ignorance [unawares, and without having a grudge against him or a reason to kill him], and unwittingly [accidentally], may flee thither, and they shall be your refuge from the avenger of blood.

Barabas continued, "We Jews can fawn like cocker spaniels when we please, and when we grin, we bite; yet our looks are as innocent and harmless as a lamb's.

"I learned in Florence, the home of Machiavelli and of Machiavellian intrigue, how to kiss my hand, shrug my shoulders when they call me dog, and bow as low as any barefoot friar, all while hoping to see them starve upon a stall — an outside bench sometimes used as a place to sleep at night by the homeless — or else to see the collection plate be passed around for them in our synagogue, so that when the offering basin comes to me for my charitable offering I may spit into it."

He looked up and said, "Here comes Don Lodowick, the Governor's son, one whom I 'love' for his 'good' father's sake."

Lodowick said, "I hear the wealthy Jew walked this way. I'll seek him out, and so insinuate myself into his favor that I may have a sight of Abigail, for Don Mathias tells me she is beautiful."

Barabas said to himself, "Now I will show myself to have more of the serpent than the dove; that is, I will be more knave than fool."

Matthew 10:16 speaks about serpents and doves: "*Behold, I send you as sheep in the midst of the wolves: be ye therefore wise as serpents, and innocent as doves*" (1599 Geneva Bible).

"Yonder walks the Jew," Lodowick said. "Now for fair Abigail."

Hearing him, Barabas said sarcastically to himself, "Aye, aye, no doubt but she's at your command."

Lodowick, who had recently shaved as preparation for seeing Abigail, walked over to Barabas and said, "Barabas, thou know I am the Governor's son."

"I wish you were his father, too, sir!" Barabas said. "That's all the harm I wish you."

Barabas seemed to others to be on good terms with Lodowick's father, Governor Ferneze, but he wanted revenge on Ferneze, whom he regarded as a bad man. By wishing that Lodowick were the father of his own father, he was wishing that Lodowick were the father of a bad son.

Deuteronomy 5:9 states, "*Thou shalt neither bow thyself unto them, nor serve them: for I the Lord thy God am a jealous God, visiting the iniquity of the fathers upon the children, even unto the third and fourth generation of them that hate me:*" (1599 Geneva Bible).

Barabas said to himself, "The freshly shaven slave looks like a newly singed hog's cheek."

"Where are you walking, Barabas?" Lodowick asked.

"No further," Barabas said. "It is a custom held with us, that when we speak with gentiles like you, we turn into the air to purge ourselves of spiritual defilement, for unto us the promise — the covenant that God gave to Abram — does belong."

This was strong language, but Barabas was able to say it because he knew that Lodowick wanted something important from him: his daughter, Abigail.

The story of the covenant God gave to Abram is told in Genesis 17, which begins in this way (1599 Geneva Bible):

1 When Abram was ninety years old and nine, the Lord appeared to Abram, and said unto him, I am God all sufficient, walk before me, and be thou upright,

2 And I will make my covenant between me and thee, and I will multiply thee exceedingly.

3 Then Abram fell on his face, and God talked with him, saying,

4 Behold, I make my covenant with thee, and thou shalt be a father of many nations,

5 Neither shall thy name anymore be called Abram, but thy name shall be Abraham: for a father of many nations have I made thee.

"Well, Barabas, can you help me to a diamond?" Lodowick asked.

"Oh, sir, your father has gotten possession of my diamonds in the past," Barabas said. "Yet I have one left that will serve your turn."

Barabas thought, *By "diamond," I mean my daughter, but before he shall have her, I'll sacrifice her on a pile of wood.*

The phrase "serve your turn" can mean "satisfy you sexually."

Barabas thought, *I have the poison of the city for Lodowick, and the white leprosy.*

"White leprosy" is a stage of leprosy in which the skin turns into slimy white scales. The "poison of the city" could possibly be plague.

2 Kings 5:27 (1599 Geneva Bible) states, "*The leprosy therefore of Naaman shall cleave unto thee, and to thy seed forever. And he went out from his presence a leper* white *as snow.*"

"What sparkle does it give without a foil?" Lodowick asked.

Thin metallic foil is set under or behind a jewel to enhance its sparkle.

"The diamond that I talk of never was foiled," Barabas said.

No jeweler had ever foiled his diamond — his daughter.

He thought, *But, when Lodowick touches it, it will be foiled.*

In this context, the word "foiled" meant "fouled or defiled." Barabas believed that his daughter would defile herself by marrying Lodowick — indeed, by marrying a Christian.

Barabas added, "Lord Lodowick, it sparkles bright and fair."

"Is it square and cube-shaped, or is it pointed?" Lodowick said. "Please, let me know."

"Pointed it is, good sir," Barabas said.

He thought, *But not for you.*

As used by Barabas, the word "pointed" meant "destined or appointed."

"I like it much the better because it is pointed," Lodowick said.

"So do I, too," Barabas said.

"How does it look at night?" Lodowick asked.

"It outshines Cynthia's — the Moon's — rays. You'll like it far better during the nights than the days."

Cynthia is the Moon-goddess.

The words "like it far better during the nights than the days" had a sexual meaning when applied to Abigail.

"And what's the price?" Lodowick asked.

Barabas thought, *Your life, if you take the diamond.*

He said out loud, "Oh, my lord, we will not quarrel about the price. Come to my house, and I will give it to your honor."

He thought, *I will give it to your honor with a vengeance.*

The phrase "give it to your honor" was used with a double meaning: 1) "give the diamond — Abigail — to you," and 2) "give you what you deserve." Barabas continued to use double meanings during his conversation with Lodowick.

"No, Barabas, I will deserve it first," Lodowick said.

"Good sir, your father has deserved it at my hands," Barabas said. "He, out of utter charity and Christian compassion, to bring me to religious purity, and, as it were, as a kind of catechizing spiritual teacher, to make me mindful of my mortal sins, against my will, and whether I would or not, seized all I had, and thrust me out of doors, and made my house a place for nuns most chaste."

A catechism summarizes the principles of Christianity in a set of questions and answers. It is often used as a form of education.

Barabas may have intended "most chaste" to modify "my house" rather than "nuns."

"No doubt your soul shall reap the fruit of it," Lodowick said.

"Aye, but, my lord, the harvest is far off," Barabas said. "And yet I know the prayers of those nuns and holy friars, having money for their pains, are wondrous —"

He thought, — *and indeed do no man good.*

Catholic nuns and friars can receive money for spiritual services such as the singing of masses and the saying of prayers.

Barabas added, "And seeing they are not idle, but still doing, it is likely they in time may reap some fruit, I mean, in fullness of perfection."

The phrase "still doing" means 1) "always working," and 2) "always sexually active."

The word "fruit" means 1) "spiritual benefits," and 2) "children."

The phrase "fullness of perfection" can mean 1) "state of perfect holiness," or 2) "pregnant and ready to give birth."

Recognizing Barabas' double meanings, Lodowick said, "Good Barabas, don't make insinuations about our holy nuns."

"No, but I do it through a burning zeal —" Barabas said.

He thought, — *hoping before long to set the house afire, for although for a while they do increase and multiply, I'll have something to say to that nunnery.*

The word "burning" can mean 1) "fervent," and 2) "incendiary."

Genesis 9:7 states, "*But bring ye forth fruit and multiply: grow plentifully in the earth, and increase therein*" (1599 Geneva Bible).

Barabas continued, "As for the diamond, sir, I told you of, come to my home, and there's no price shall make us part, even for your honorable father's sake."

He thought, *It shall go hard but I will see your death.*

He added, "But now I must be gone to buy a slave."

"And, Barabas, I'll bear thee company," Lodowick said.

"Come then," Barabas said. "Here's the marketplace."

Looking at a Turk for sale, Barabas asked the first officer, "What's the price of this slave, 200 crowns — 200 gold coins? Is that his weight? Do the Turks weigh so much?"

"Sir, that's his price," the first officer said.

"What!" Barabas said. "Can he steal, and that's why you demand so much money for him? Probably he has some new trick for stealing a purse. If he has, he is worth three hundred plates — Spanish silver coins — as long as, once he is bought, the town seal might be gotten to keep him for his lifetime away from the gallows."

Barabas meant that the slave would be worth the asking price if he could steal without the risk of being caught, tried in court, and then hung. This could be done if the slave, once bought, stole the town seal — with it, the slave's owner could create an official pardon for the slave's crimes.

Barabas continued, "The trial-day is critical to thieves, and few or none escape except by being purged."

A critical day in an illness is a dangerous day during which the patient could die. A critical day for a thief is the day spent in court. In this society, many thieves were found guilty and were hung.

The word "purging" may refer to being cleared of the crime. This would be an escape from the court.

The word "purging," however, does have a medical meaning and a religious meaning that would result in or be a result of an "escape" from the court:

1) Being purged by a "doctor" who hopes to cure the "patient." One such cure was to induce vomiting or evacuation of the patient's bowels; although this was intended to lead to a cure, it sometimes resulted in the death of the patient. The purging of the thief was often his being hung — this cured the thief of being a thief.

2) Being punished for sins on the Mountain of Purgatory after death. This leads to being purged of those sins.

Looking at a Moor — a North African — for sale, Lodowick asked, "Do thou price this Moor only at 200 plates — Spanish silver coins?"

"No more, my lord," the first officer said.

"Why should this Turk be more expensive than that Moor?" Barabas asked.

"Because he is young and has more abilities," the first officer answered.

Barabas asked the Turk, "What! Do you have the philosopher's stone? If thou have it, break my head with it — I'll forgive thee."

Some people believed that the philosopher's stone could make gold out of base metals such as lead. Getting hit in the head was a small price to pay for the philosopher's stone.

"No, sir," the Turkish slave said. "I can cut and shave."

"Let me see, sirrah," Barabas asked. "Aren't you an old shaver?"

A shaver can be 1) "a barber," 2) "a fellow," or 3) "a rogue or conman."

The Turkish slave answered, "Alas, sir, I am really a youth."

"A youth?" Barabas said. "I'll buy you and marry you to Lady Vanity, if you do well."

When Youth is married to Vanity, the results are bad.

The Turkish slave said, "I will serve you, sir —"

Barabas interrupted, "— some wicked trick or other. It may be that under pretext of shaving me, thou shall cut my throat for my goods.

"Tell me, do you have good health?"

"Aye, I am very well in health," the Turkish slave answered.

"So much the worse," Barabas said. "I must have a slave who is sickly, if only to save on money for feeding him. Not even a stone — fourteen pounds — of beef a day will maintain you and your fat cheeks."

He said to the first officer, "Let me see a slave who's somewhat leaner."

"Here's one who is leaner," the first officer said. "How do you like him?"

"Where were thou born?" Barabas asked the leaner slave, whose name was Ithamore.

"In Thrace," Ithamore answered. "I was brought up in Arabia."

The Turkish Empire included part of the region that is now Saudi Arabia.

"So much the better," Barabas said. "Thou are for my turn — you'll do."

He said to the first officer, "The price is a hundred crowns? I'll have him; there's the money."

Barabas handed over the money.

The first officer took the money and said, "Now mark him as yours, sir, and take him away from here."

Barabas thought, *Aye, mark him, you were best; keep an eye on him, for this is he who with my help shall do much villainy.*

He said to Lodowick, "My lord, farewell."

He said to Ithamore, "Come, sirrah, you are my slave now."

Mathias and his mother, whose name was Katherine, arrived at the slave market.

Barabas said to Lodowick, "As for the diamond, it shall be yours. Please, sir, don't be a stranger at my house. All that I have shall be at your command."

Seeing Barabas talking to Lodowick, Mathias thought, *What makes the Jew and Lodowick so private? I am afraid that they are talking privately about fair Abigail.*

Lodowick exited.

Barabas said to Ithamore, "Yonder comes Don Mathias. Let us stop here. He loves my daughter, and she holds him dear, but I have sworn to frustrate both their hopes, and be revenged upon the" — he paused for emphasis — "Governor."

Barabas was talking openly to Ithamore about his plans. Because Ithamore was from Thrace, and the Thracians were famous for cruelty, Ithamore was a good person to assist Barabas in getting revenge.

Katherine said to Mathias, "This Moor is very attractive, isn't he? Do you agree, son?"

"No, this slave is better, mother," Mathias said. "Look carefully at this one."

Barabas whispered to Mathias, "Pretend not to know me here before your mother, lest she suspect the match that is in hand. When you have escorted your mother home, come to my house. Think of me as thy father. Son, farewell."

Mathias whispered to Barabas, "But why did Don Lodowick talk with you?"

Barabas whispered back, "Tush, man, we talked about diamonds, not of Abigail."

"Tell me, Mathias," Katherine said, "isn't that the Jew?"

Pretending that he and Mathias had been talking about a book, Barabas said out loud, "As for the commentary on the first and second books of Maccabees, I have it, sir, and it is at your command. You can borrow it."

"Yes, madam," Mathias said, "and my talk with him was about the borrowing of a book or two."

"Don't talk with him," Katherine said. "He is cast off from heaven."

Katherine gave money to the first officer to buy a slave, saying, "Thou have thy crowns, fellow."

She then said to Mathias, "Come, let's leave."

"Sirrah Jew, remember the book," Mathias said.

"Indeed, I will, sir," Barabas replied.

Katherine and Mathias left, accompanied by the slave whom Katherine had bought.

The first officer said to the other officers, "Come, I have made a reasonable market. Let's leave."

The officers and the remaining slaves left.

Barabas and Ithamore began walking to Barabas' home, which was nearby.

Barabas said to Ithamore, "Now let me know thy name, and also your birth, character, and profession."

"Indeed, sir, my birth is low, and my name's Ithamore. My profession is whatever you please."

He was willing to do whatever Barabas wanted, and so by telling Barabas, "My profession is what you please," he was also telling him about his character.

"Have thou no trade?" Barabas said. "Then listen to my words, and I will teach thee something worthwhile that shall stick by thee. First, be thou void of these emotions: compassion, love, vain hope, and cowardly fear. Be moved at nothing. See thou pity none, but to thyself smile when the Christians moan."

"Oh, splendid master!" Ithamore said. "I worship your nose for this."

Barabas had a large nose.

"As for myself," Barabas said, "I walk abroad at night and kill sick people groaning under walls. Sometimes I go about and poison wells, and now and then, to encourage Christian thieves, I am content to lose some of my crowns in a trap for thieves so that I may, walking in my upper gallery, see them captured and go with bound arms along by my door.

"When I was young, I studied medicine, and began to practice first upon the Italians. There I enriched the priests with burials and always kept the sexton's arms in use with digging graves and ringing knells to announce the deaths of men.

"And after that I was an engineer who constructed military devices, and in the wars between France and Germany, under pretense of helping Holy Roman Emperor Charles the Fifth fight against King Francis the First of France, I slew both friends and enemies with my stratagems.

"After that I was a usurious moneylender, and with extorting, cheating, causing borrowers to forfeit their property because of failure to repay a loan, and employing tricks belonging to dishonest brokers, I filled the jails with bankrupts in a year, and I placed young orphans in charitable institutions, and every moon — every month — I made someone or other insane, and now and then I caused someone to hang himself for grief after he pinned upon his breast a long great scroll about how I tormented him with the interest I charged him for loans."

Barabas could force forfeiture if someone could not pay the interest on a loan.

He continued, "But note how I am blest for plaguing them. I have as much money as will buy the town.

"But tell me now, how have thou spent thy time?"

"Indeed, master," Ithamore said. "I have spent my time in setting Christian villages on fire, chaining eunuchs, and binding galley slaves.

"Once I was a stable-man at an inn, and in the nighttime secretly I would steal into travellers' chambers, and there cut their throats.

"Once at Jerusalem, where the pilgrims kneeled, I strewed powder on the marble stones, and because of this powder their knees would so fester that I have laughed heartily to see the cripples go limping home to Christendom on crutches."

"Why, this is something," Barabas said. "Consider me your friend. We are both villains. We are both circumcised. We both hate Christians.

"Be true to me and secret; thou shall lack no gold.

"But stand to the side. Here comes Don Lodowick."

Lodowick walked over to Barabas and said, "Oh, Barabas, we are well met. Where is the diamond you told me of?"

"I have it for you, sir," Barabas said. "Please walk in my house with me."

He called, "Abigail! Open the door, I say."

Abigail opened the door and came outside.

"You have come at a good time, father. Here are letters come from the city of Ormus, and the messenger waits inside here."

Located at the mouth of the Persian Gulf, the city of Ormus engaged in much trade.

"Give me the letters," Barabas said.

She gave him the letters.

Barabas said, "Daughter, listen to me. Entertain Lodowick, the Governor's son, with all the courtesy you can manage."

He then whispered so Lodowick could not hear him, "That is, with all the courtesy you can manage provided that you keep your virginity. Treat him as if he were a Philistine."

The Philistines were in conflict with the Jews in the Old Testament. Goliath was a Philistine.

Barabas continued whispering to his daughter, "Lie, swear, profess that you like him, vow love to him. He is not of the seed of Abraham."

He said to Lodowick, "I am a little busy, sir; please, pardon me."

He said out loud to his daughter, "Abigail, tell Lodowick he's welcome for my sake."

"For your sake and his own, he's welcome here," Abigail said.

Barabas whispered to Abigail, "Daughter, a word more. Kiss him, speak courteously to him, and like a cunning Jew so devise that you two are betrothed to each other before you come out of the house."

Abigail whispered, "Oh, father, Don Mathias is my love."

Barabas whispered, "I know it. Yet I say flirt with Lodowick and be irresistible. Do it — it is necessary that it should be done."

Loudly, pretending that he and Abigail had been discussing the letters, Barabas said, "Nay, on my life, it is my agent's handwriting."

He then said to Abigail and Lodowick, "But you two go in. I'll think upon the account."

Lodowick thought he meant the business account mentioned in the letters.

Abigail and Lodowick went inside Barabas' house.

Barabas said, "The account — the settling of scores — is made, for Lodowick dies."

Referring to the letters, he said, "My agent sends me word that a merchant has fled who owes me for a hundred barrels of wine. I weigh it thus much" — he snapped his fingers — "I have enough wealth."

He then said, "Now by this time Lodowick has kissed Abigail, and she vows love to him and he to her. As surely as heaven rained manna for the Jews, so surely shall Lodowick and Don Mathias die. Lodowick's father was my chiefest enemy when as Governor he seized my property."

Exodus 16:14-15 (1599 Geneva Bible) states this:

14 And when the dew that was fallen was ascended, behold, a small round thing was upon the face of the wilderness, small as the hoary frost upon the earth.

15 And when the children of Israel saw it, they said one to another, It is Manna, for they wist not what it was. And Moses said unto them, This is the bread which the Lord hath given you to eat.

Mathias arrived.

Seeing him, Barabas said, "Where is Don Mathias going? Stay here a while."

"Where should I be going but to my fair love, Abigail?" Mathias said.

"Thou know, and heaven can witness that it is true," Barabas said, "that I intend my daughter shall be thine."

"Aye, Barabas, or else thou wrong me much," Mathias said.

"Oh, heaven forbid I should have such a thought," Barabas said. "Pardon me although I weep. Lodowick, the Governor's son, will, whether or not I am willing, have Abigail. He sends her letters, bracelets, jewels, rings."

"Does she accept them?" Mathias asked.

"She?" Barabas said. "No, Mathias, no. Instead, she sends them back, and, when he comes, she locks herself up securely. Yet through the keyhole he will talk to her, while she runs to the window, looking out to see when you should come and drag him from the door."

"Oh, treacherous Lodowick!" Mathias said.

"Just now, as I came home, he slipped in past me," Barabas said, "and I am sure he is with Abigail."

"I'll rouse him away from there," Mathias said.

To rouse a game animal is to force it out of hiding. Mathias now regarded Lodowick as less than human.

"Not for all Malta; therefore, sheathe your sword," Barabas said. "If you love and respect me, have no quarrels in my house, but sneak into my house, and pretend not to see him — avoid him.

"I'll give him such a warning before he goes that he shall have small hopes of Abigail."

Mathias did not have time to go in Barabas' house at this time because Lodowick and Abigail came outside, holding hands.

Barabas said to Mathias, "Go, for here they come."

"What, hand in hand!" Mathias said. "I cannot endure this!"

"Mathias, as thou love me, don't say a word," Barabas said.

"Well, let it pass," Mathias said. "Another time shall serve."

Mathias exited.

"Barabas, isn't that the widow's son?" Lodowick asked.

"Aye, and take heed, for he has sworn your death."

"My death? What! Is the base-born peasant mad?"

"No, no," Barabas said, "but perhaps he stands in fear of that which you, I think, never dream upon — my daughter here, a paltry, unsophisticated girl."

"Why, does she love Don Mathias?" Lodowick asked.

"Doesn't she with her smiling at you answer that question?" Barabas replied.

Abigail thought, *Mathias has my heart. I smile against my will.*

"Barabas, thou know that I have long loved thy daughter," Lodowick said.

Actually, this was the first time he had seen her, at least since she was a child.

Barabas lied, "And so has she loved you, even from when she was a child."

"And now I can no longer hold back from expressing my mind," Lodowick said.

"Nor can I hold back the 'affection' that I bear to you," Barabas said.

"This is thy diamond," Lodowick said. "Tell me, shall I have it?"

"Win it, and wear it," Barabas said. "It is yet unfoiled."

"Unfoiled" means 1) "without a foil — in this case, a husband — to set it off," 2) "unsullied," 3) "virginal," and 4) "unplowed."

To Barabas, if Abigail were to marry a gentile such as Lodowick, she would be sullied.

Barabas continued, "Oh, but I know your lordship would disdain to marry the daughter of a Jew, and yet I'll give her many a golden coin decorated with crosses and with Christian posies inscribed round about the edge of the coins."

This was an insult. Barabas was saying that Lodowick would not marry a Jew — except for money.

"Christian posies" are pious short sayings or mottos.

"It is not thy wealth, but her whom I esteem," Lodowick said. "Yet I crave thy consent."

Barabas would show he consented by giving a dowry to Lodowick.

"And my consent you have; yet let me talk to her," Barabas said.

He whispered to Abigail, "This offspring of Cain, this Jebusite who never tasted of the Passover, nor shall ever see the land of Canaan nor our Messiah Who is yet to come, this gentle — well-born and gentile — maggot, Lodowick, I mean, must be deluded."

Cain is the first murderer; he murdered Abel, his brother. The Jebusites lived in Jerusalem before King David captured it. They did not worship the one true God.

In this culture, one meaning of the noun "gentle" is "maggot." According to the *Oxford English Dictionary*, "gentle" can mean "A larva of a blowfly (family Calliphoridae), esp. the bluebottle, Calliphora vomitoria, used as bait."

Barabas said out loud to his daughter, "Let him have thy hand."

He whispered to her, "But keep thy heart until Don Mathias comes."

Abigail whispered to her father, "What! Shall I be betrothed to Lodowick?"

Barabas whispered back, "It's no sin to deceive a Christian, for they themselves hold as a principle that faith is not to be held with heretics — that Christians need not keep their promises to heretics."

On 6 July 1415, Jan Huss was burned at the stake although Catholics had promised him safe conduct; the Catholics excused the breaking of their promise by saying that Jan Hus was a heretic.

Barabas continued whispering to Abigail, "But all who are not Jews are heretics. This follows well and logically, and therefore, daughter, don't be afraid to break your promise to a Christian."

He said out loud to Lodowick, "I have entreated her, and she will agree to be your wife."

"Then, gentle Abigail, plight thy faith and become betrothed to me," Lodowick said.

Abigail thought, *I cannot choose what I want, seeing my father tells me to do otherwise.*

The vow of betrothal in this culture was a serious, binding vow. Two betrothed people would be married.

Abigail said to Lodowick, "Nothing but death shall part my love and me."

Lodowick thought that "my love" referred to him, but Abigail used "my love" to refer to Mathias.

"Now I have that for which my soul has longed," Lodowick said.

Barabas thought, *That is something I don't have; but yet I hope I shall.*

Abigail thought, *Oh wretched Abigail, what have thou done?*

Lodowick asked her, "Why has your color changed suddenly?"

"I don't know," Abigail replied. "But farewell; I must leave."

Barabas whispered to Ithamore, "Stop her from leaving, but don't let her speak one more word."

Abigail overheard him.

Ithamore took her to one side. If necessary to keep her quiet, he would put his hand over her mouth; however, Abigail was an obedient daughter and kept quiet, although some tears trickled down her face.

"Mute all of the sudden!" Lodowick said. "Here's a sudden change."

"Oh, don't wonder at it," Barabas said, "It is the Hebrew custom that maidens newly betrothed should weep a while. Don't trouble her. Sweet Lodowick, depart. She is thy wife, and thou shall be my heir."

"Oh, is it the custom?" Lodowick said. "Then I am satisfied. But rather let the brightsome heavens be dim, and nature's beauty choke with stifling clouds, than my fair Abigail should frown on me."

He saw Mathias coming, and he said, "There comes the villain; now I'll be revenged."

"Be calm and quiet, Lodowick," Barabas said. "It is enough that I have made thee sure — engaged — to Abigail."

"Well, let him go," Lodowick said, and he left the house.

Mathias walked over to Barabas.

Barabas whispered to Mathias, "Well, if not for me, as you went in at these doors you would have been stabbed, but not a word about it now. Here must no speeches pass, nor swords be drawn."

"Allow me, Barabas, to follow him," Mathias said.

"No," Barabas said. "If you follow him, I shall, if any hurt would be done, be made an accessory of your deeds. Get revenge on him when you next meet him."

"For this I'll have his heart," Mathias said.

"Do that," Barabas said. "Lo, here I give thee Abigail."

"What greater gift can poor Mathias have?" Mathias said. "Shall Lodowick rob me of so fair a love? My life is not as dear to me as is Abigail."

"My heart makes me afraid that to thwart your love he's with your mother," Barabas said. "Therefore, go after him."

"Has he gone to my mother?" Mathias asked.

"If you want to, stay here until she comes herself," Barabas said.

"I cannot stay," Mathias said, "for, if my mother comes, she'll die with grief."

She would die with grief because her son was marrying a Jew.

Mathias exited.

"I cannot say goodbye to him because of my tears," Abigail said. "Father, why have you thus incensed them both?"

"What's that to thee?" Barabas said.

"I'll make them friends again," Abigail said.

"You'll make them friends?" Barabas said. "Aren't there Jews enough in Malta? Must thou dote upon a Christian?"

"I will have Don Mathias," Abigail said. "He is my love."

"Yes, you shall have him," Barabas lied.

He ordered Ithamore, "Go put her in the house."

"Aye, I'll put her in," Ithamore replied.

He pushed Abigail into the house.

"Now tell me, Ithamore," Barabas said, "how do thou like this? What do you think about what you have heard and seen?"

"Indeed, master, I think that by doing this you will obtain both their lives — you are plotting to bring about both of their deaths," Ithamore said. "Isn't that true?"

"True, and it shall be cunningly performed."

"Oh, master, I wish that I might have a hand in this!"

"Aye, so thou shall; it is thou who must do the deed," Barabas said. "Take this letter and carry it to Mathias immediately, and tell him that it comes from Lodowick."

"It is scented with poisoned perfume, isn't it?" Mathias asked.

"No, no; and yet my goal might be accomplished that way," Barabas said. "It is a feigned challenge from Lodowick."

"Fear not. I will so set his heart on fire that Mathias shall truly think it comes from Lodowick."

"I cannot choose but like thy readiness," Barabas said. "Yet don't be rash, but do this cunningly."

"As I behave myself in this, employ me hereafter," Ithamore said, and then he exited.

"Away, then!" Barabas said to the departing Ithamore.

He then said to himself, "So, now I will go to Lodowick, and, like a cunning devil, feign some lie until I have set them both at enmity."

CHAPTER 3

— 3.1 —

Bellamira, a courtesan, was complaining about the Turkish fleet that was near Malta. It had a bad effect on her profits; for one thing, much money had been collected to pay the tribute, thus reducing disposable income that could be spent on her.

She said to herself, "Since this town was besieged, my gain grows cold — my profits are low. The time has been that but for one bare — single and naked — night with me a hundred gold coins have been freely given, but now against my will I must be chaste. And yet I know that my beauty does not fail. From Venice merchants, and from Padua rare-witted gentlemen — scholars, I mean, learned and liberal — were accustomed to come to me."

"Liberal" means 1) "well-educated" and 2) "generous."

She continued, "And now, except for Pilia-Borza, there comes no one. Pilia-Borza is very seldom away from my house — and here he comes."

Pilia-Borza arrived on the scene.

"Hold out your hand, wench," he said.

He put a moneybag in her hand and said, "There's something for thee to spend."

Bellamira looked in the moneybag and said, "It is silver. I disdain it."

"Aye, but the Jew has gold, and I will have it, or it shall go hard," Pilia-Borza said.

"Tell me, how came thou by this information?" Bellamira asked.

He replied, "Indeed, walking the back lanes, through the gardens, I chanced to cast my eye up to the Jew's counting-house, where I saw some bags of money, and in the night I clambered up with my hooks; and, as I was taking my choice of moneybags, I heard a rumbling in the house; so I took only this one, and ran on my way."

Thieves carried a staff that had a hook at one end. Pilia-Borza had climbed up to Barabas' window and then had used his staff to hook and steal one of the moneybags. Possibly, he also had hooks to help him climb.

He said, "But here comes the Jew's man."

By "man," he meant "man-servant."

Ithamore arrived on the scene.

"Hide the bag," Bellamira said.

"Don't look towards him," Pilia-Borza said. "Let's go. By God's wounds, what staring thou keep making toward him! Thou will betray us immediately."

Bellamira and Pilia-Borza exited.

Ithamore said about Bellamira, "Oh, the sweetest face that I ever beheld! I know she is a courtesan by her attire. Now I would give a hundred of the Jew's crowns so that I would have such a concubine. Well, I have delivered Barabas' forged challenge to Mathias in such a way that he and Lodowick will meet and die fighting — this is excellent entertainment!"

Alone, Mathias arrived at the place that the forged letter — supposedly from Lodowick — had appointed for a duel.

He said to himself, "This is the place. Now Abigail shall see whether or not Mathias regards her as dear."

Lodowick arrived, reading a letter that Mathias had written after reading the forged letter that he believed that Lodowick had written.

He said, "Does the villain dare write in such base terms?"

"I did it — and revenge it, if thou dare," Mathias said.

The two men drew their swords and began to fight the duel.

Barabas arrived and watched the duel, saying, "Oh, bravely fought! And yet they thrust not home — to the heart. Now, Lodowick! Now, Mathias! So!"

Lodowick and Mathias wounded each other mortally, fell, and died.

"So, now they have showed themselves to be 'splendid' fellows," Barabas said.

Voices called out as people ran to the duel, "Part them! Part them!"

"Aye, part them, now they are dead," Barabas said. "Farewell, farewell."

He exited.

Governor Ferneze and Mathias' mother — Katherine — arrived, as did some attendants.

"What a sight this is!" Governor Ferneze said. "My Lodowick slain! These arms of mine shall be thy sepulcher."

"Who is this?" Katherine said, looking at a corpse. "My son, Mathias, slain!"

"Oh, Lodowick, if thou had perished by the Turk, I, wretched Ferneze, might have avenged thy death!"

Governor Ferneze could not get revenge by killing Mathias because Mathias was dead. He also could not get revenge by killing Mathias' next of kin because Mathias' next of kin was a woman: his mother.

"Thy son slew mine, and I'll revenge his death," Katherine said to Governor Ferneze.

"Look, Katherine, look! Thy son gave mine these wounds."

"Oh, cease to grieve me," Katherine said. "I am grieved enough."

"Oh, I wish that my sighs could turn to life-giving breath, and these my tears could turn to blood, so that my son might live," Governor Ferneze said.

"Who made them enemies?" Katherine asked.

"I don't know, and that grieves me most of all."

"My son loved and respected your son."

"And so did Lodowick love and respect your son."

"Lend me that weapon that killed my son, and it shall murder me," Katherine said.

"Nay, madam, stay," Governor Ferneze said. "That weapon was my son's, and on that weapon I, Ferneze, am the one who should die."

"Wait," Katherine said. "Let's inquire about who were the causers of their deaths, so that we may avenge our sons' blood upon the murderers' heads."

Governor Ferneze ordered, "Take up their corpses, and let them be interred within one sacred monument of stone, upon which altar I will offer up my daily sacrifice of sighs and tears, and with my prayers I will pierce the indifferent heavens until they reveal the causers of our sorrows — those who forced our sons' hands to divide united hearts.

"Come, Katherine, our losses are equal, so then of true grief let us take an equal share."

Alone, Ithamore said to himself, "Why, was there ever seen such villainy so neatly plotted, and so well performed? Both Mathias and Lodowick were held in hand and led on, and both were completely beguiled!"

He laughed.

Abigail arrived, saw him, and asked, "Why, how are you now, Ithamore? Why do thou laugh so?

"Oh, mistress! Ha! Ha! Ha!"

"Why, what is wrong with thou?"

"Oh, my master!"

"Huh?"

"Oh, mistress, I have the most splendid, gravest, most secret and subtle, big-nosed knave for my master that any gentleman has ever had."

"Tell me, knave," Abigail asked, "why do you mock my father like this?"

"Oh, my master has the most splendid and most cunning policy," Ithamore said.

"Policy to accomplish what?"

"Why, don't you know?"

"Why, no."

"Don't you know about Mathias' and Don Lodowick's disaster?"

"No," Abigail said. "What was it?"

"Why, the devil invented a challenge, my master wrote it, and I carried it, first to Lodowick, and *imprimis* to Mathias," Ithamore said.

Imprimis is Latin for "in the first place," and so Ithamore apparently didn't know Latin. Ithamore had carried a forged challenge to Mathias, and then had carried Mathias' reply to Lodowick. Mathias did not know that the challenge from "Lodowick" he had read had been forged, and Lodowick did not know that Mathias' insulting letter to him was in reply to a forged challenge that Mathias had thought came from Lodowick.

Possibly, however, when Barabas had given him the written challenge, Ithamore had changed Barabas' plot by making a copy of the challenge (changing names as necessary) and giving it to Lodowick, telling him that it had come from Mathias, his rival for Abigail. He then had given the *imprimis* (first and original) challenge to Mathias, saying that it had come from Lodowick. In this case, Ithamore may think that "*imprimis*" means "next." He then had given Lodowick Mathias' real reply to the forged challenge.

Ithamore continued, "And then they met, and as the story says, in doleful wise they ended both their days. They died."

"And was my father the furtherer of their deaths?" Abigail asked.

"Am I Ithamore?"

"Yes."

"As surely as I am Ithamore, your father wrote the challenge and I carried it."

"Well, Ithamore, let me request that thee do this: Go to the new-made nunnery, and inquire for any of the friars of Saint Jacques, and tell them that I ask any of them to please come and speak with me."

The friars of Saint Jacques were Dominicans. They were also called Jacobins because the Church of St. Jacques (in Latin, Saint Jacobus, aka Saint James) in Paris had been given to them. Near this church, they built their first monastery.

"I ask you, mistress, will you answer me one question?" Ithamore asked.

"Well, sirrah, what is it?"

"A very feeling one," Ithamore said.

The word "feeling" means 1) "deeply felt" and 2) "erotic."

He continued, "Don't the nuns have fine sport — sex — with the friars now and then?"

"Bah, Sirrah Saucy Fellow!" Abigail said. "Is this your question? Get thee gone!"

"I will, indeed, mistress."

Ithamore exited.

"Hardhearted father, unkind Barabas, was this the purpose of thy policy?" Abigail said to herself.

In addition to the usual meaning, in this culture the word "unkind" meant "unnatural." A father should naturally care for his children, but Abigail's father, Barabas, had greatly hurt her by causing the death of Mathias, the man she loved.

She continued, "Was your cunning plan to make me show favor to them separately, so that because of their love for me they should both be slain?

"Granted that thou did not love Lodowick because of his sire, yet Don Mathias never offended thee. But thou were set upon extreme revenge because the Prior" — the Governor of Malta is the Grand Prior of the Knights of Malta — "dispossessed thee once, and you could not revenge it except upon his son, Lodowick. Nor could you revenge it on Lodowick except by means of using Mathias, nor could you use Mathias to accomplish your purpose except by getting him killed and thereby murdering me.

"But I perceive there is no love on earth, no pity in Jews, nor any piety in Turks.

"But here comes cursed Ithamore with the friar."

Ithamore and Friar Jacomo walked over to Abigail.

Friar Jacomo bowed to Abigail and said, "*Virgo, salve.*"

The Latin means "Hail, maiden!"

Abigail curtsied.

Disgusted by a Jew showing courtesy to a Christian — Ithamore hated Christians — Ithamore said to her, "You duck, do you?"

"Welcome, grave friar," Abigail said.

She then said, "Ithamore, be gone."

Ithamore exited.

Abigail said to Friar Jacomo, "Know, holy sir, that I am bold to solicit thee."

"To do what?"

"To get me admitted as a nun."

"Why, Abigail, it is not yet long since I labored to arrange thy admission to the nunnery, and then thou did not like that holy life," Friar Jacomo said.

"At that time my thoughts were so frail and unsettled because I was chained to follies of the world, but now experience, purchased with grief, has made me see the difference of things," Abigail replied. "My sinful soul, alas, has paced too long the fatal labyrinth of misbelief, far from the Son — Jesus Christ — Who gives eternal life."

"Who taught thee this?" Friar Jacomo asked.

"The abbess of the house, whose zealous counsel I embrace. Oh, therefore, Jacomo, let me be one, although unworthy, of that sisterhood."

"Abigail, I will. But see thou change no more, for that will be most grievous to thy soul."

"That was my father's fault," Abigail said.

"Thy father's? How?"

"Nay, you shall pardon me for not telling you that."

She thought, *Oh, Barabas, though thou deserve severity at my hands, yet never shall these lips betray secrets that will endanger thy life.*

"Come, shall we go?" Friar Jacomo asked.

"My duty waits on you," Abigail said. "I will follow you."

Barabas sat in a room in his home, reading a letter.

"What! Abigail has become a nun again!" he said. "False and unkind! Have thou abandoned and lost thy father? And, all unknown and unconstrained by me, have thou again got to the nunnery?

"Now here she writes, and wishes me to repent.

"Repentance? *Spurca!*"

"*Spurca*" is the feminine form of the Latin adjective for "filthy." "*Paenitentia*" is a Latin noun meaning "repentance"; it has a feminine form. (The Italian noun meaning "repentance" is "*pentimento*," which is masculine.)

Barabas was calling repentance — not his daughter — filthy. This kind of repentance, of course, means converting to Christianity.

He continued, "What is the meaning of this?

"I fear she knows — I see that it is so — of my plot that resulted in Don Mathias' and Lodowick's deaths.

"If so, it is time that it is looked into and dealt with, for she who varies from me in belief gives great grounds for presuming that she does not love me, or, if she still loves me, she dislikes something I have done."

Ithamore entered the room.

"But who comes here?" Barabas said. "Oh, Ithamore, come near. Come near, my love; come near, thy master's life, my trusty servant, nay, my second life, for I have now no hope except in thee, and on that hope my happiness is built.

"When did thou last see Abigail?"

"Today."

"With whom?"

"A friar."

"A friar!" Barabas said. "False villain, he has done the deed."

"What, sir?" Ithamore asked.

"Why, the friar has made my Abigail a nun."

"That's no lie, for she sent me for him," Ithamore said.

One meaning of "done the deed" is "have sex with." Both Barabas and Ithamore believed that friars and nuns commonly have sex.

"Oh, unhappy day!" Barabas said. "False, credulous, inconstant Abigail! But let them go. And, Ithamore, from henceforward never shall she grieve me more with her disgrace. Never shall she live to inherit anything of mine. Never shall she be blest by me, nor come within my gates, but instead she shall perish underneath my bitter curse, like Cain by Adam, for his brother's death."

Actually, it was God Who cursed Cain after Cain murdered Abel, his brother. Although God cursed Cain, He also protected him by marking him so that others would not kill him. This story is told in Genesis 4.

"Oh, master!"

"Ithamore, don't beg in behalf of her. I am angry, and she is hateful to my soul and me, and, lest thou yield to this that I entreat you to do, I cannot think but that thou hate my life."

"Who, I, master?" Ithamore said. "Why, I'll run to some rock, and throw myself headlong into the sea. Why, I'll do anything for your sweet sake."

"Oh, trusty Ithamore, you are no servant, but my friend. I here adopt thee for my only heir. All that I have is thine — when I am dead. And while I live use half. Spend as if you were myself. Here, take my keys. Go buy thee garments."

He held out his keys but then drew them to himself again, saying, "I'll give them to thee soon."

He then said, "But thou shall not lack. Only know this — that thus thou are to do in the future."

In other words, in the future — but not now — Ithamore could spend half of Barabas' money and buy garments.

Barabas said, "But first go and fetch me the pot of rice that for our supper stands upon the fire."

Ithamore thought, *I bet my head that my master's hungry.*

He said out loud, "I go, sir."

He exited.

Barabas said to himself, "Thus every villain ambles after wealth, although he never becomes richer except in hope."

In other words, Barabas most likely had no intention of allowing Ithamore to spend any of his money but was simply manipulating him by making him think he could soon spend Barabas' money.

Hearing Ithamore returning, Barabas said to himself, "But, hush!"

Ithamore returned, carrying the cooking pot.

"Here it is, master."

"Well done, Ithamore. What, have thou brought the ladle with thee, too?"

"Yes, sir," Ithamore said. "The proverb says that he who eats with the devil has need of a long spoon. I have brought you a ladle."

Perhaps Ithamore should have brought a ladle for himself.

"Very well, Ithamore," Barabas said. "Then now be secret, and for thy sake, whom I so dearly love, now shall thou see the death of Abigail, with the result that thou may freely live to be my heir."

"Why, master, will you 'poison' her with a serving of rice porridge? That will preserve her life, make her round and plump, and make her thrive more than you are aware."

"Aye, but Ithamore, do thou see this?" Barabas said, holding up a small container. "It is a precious powder that I bought from an Italian in Ancona once."

Ancona was an Italian port whose inhabitants were tolerant toward Jews, but beginning in 1555, Pope Paul IV persecuted the Jews there. Twenty-three Jews who refused to convert to Christianity were hanged. Similarly, Barabas once loved his daughter, but now he wanted to kill her.

Italians had an international reputation as poisoners.

Barabas continued, "The effects of this poison are to bind the bowels, infect, and poison deeply, yet not appear until forty hours after it is taken."

"How will you poison her, master?"

"In this way, Ithamore," Barabas said. "This evening there is a custom in Malta here — it is called Saint Jacques' Eve — and then, I say, the Maltese are accustomed to send their alms to the nunneries. Among the others who are bringing food offerings, carry this, and set it there. There's a dark entry where they take it in, where they must neither see the messenger, nor make inquiry into who has sent it to them."

"Why?"

"Probably it is some customary observance," Barabas said. "There, Ithamore, must thou go and place this pot. Wait. Let me 'season' it first."

"Please do, and let me help you, master," Ithamore said. "Please, let me taste it first."

"Go ahead."

Ithamore tasted the food.

Barabas asked, "What do you say now?"

"Truly, master, I'm loath such a pot of pottage should be spoiled."

"Pottage" can be 1) "soup," 2) "stew," or 3) "porridge."

Barabas put in the poison and said, "Peace, Ithamore. It is better so than spared."

He meant these things: 1) "It is better that we poison the food for this purpose than to spare it and eat it ourselves," and 2) "It is better to do this than spare the lives of Abigail and the other nuns." He may have also been sardonically referring to Proverbs 13:24: "*He that spareth his rod, hateth his son: but he that loveth him chasteneth him betime*" (1599 Geneva Bible).

He added, "Assure thyself thou shall have broth — as much as your eye desires. My purse, my coffer, and myself are thine."

"Well, master, I go," Ithamore said.

"Wait! First let me stir it, Ithamore."

Barabas stirred the poison to mix it with the food and then said, "As fatal may it be to her as the draught of wine that great Alexander drank and from which he died, and with her let it work like Borgia's wine with which his sire, the Pope, was poisoned."

These are historical inaccuracies. Alexander the Great did not die after drinking poisoned wine that Antipater, his general, supposedly gave him, and Pope Alexander VI did not die after drinking poisoned wine that Cesare Borgia, his son, had supposedly prepared to be drunk by someone else.

Barabas continued, "In short, may the blood of Hydra, the bane and plague of Lerna, the juice of hebon, and Cocytus' breath, and all the poisons of the Stygian pool break from the fiery kingdom of Hell, and in this food vomit your venom and envenom her who like a fiend has left her father thus!"

The Lernaean Hydra was a nine-headed water-snake with poisonous blood that Hercules killed as one of his famous labors. Hebon is a poisonous plant. Cocytus and Styx ("the Stygian pool") are rivers in the Land of the Dead. Their breath — vapor — was regarded as harmful.

Ithamore thought, *What a blessing has he given it! Was ever a pot of rice porridge so seasoned?*

He asked out loud, "What shall I do with it?"

"Oh my sweet Ithamore, go and set it down, and come again as soon as thou hast done, for I have other business for thee."

"Here's a drench to poison a whole stable of Flanders mares," Ithamore said.

A drench is a dose of medicine given to a horse. A Flanders mare is either a Belgian horse or a lascivious woman. Ithamore regarded the nuns as lascivious women. Flanders mares were bred, and according to Ithamore, so were nuns.

He added, "I'll carry it to the nuns with a powder."

"With a powder" means "with great haste," but Ithamore also had in mind the poisonous powder that Barabas had put in the food.

Barabas said, "And infect the nuns with the horse pestilence as well. Away!"

"I am gone," Ithamore said. "Pay me my wages, for my work is done."

He exited.

Barabas said, "I'll pay thee with a vengeance, Ithamore."

Governor Ferneze; Martin del Bosco, the Spanish Vice-Admiral; and some Knights of Malta were meeting with a Turkish Pasha.

"Welcome, great Pasha," Governor Ferneze said. "How fares Calymath? What wind drives you thus into Malta harbor?"

"The wind that blows all the world besides: desire of gold," the Pasha said.

"Desire of gold, great sir? That's to be gotten in the Western Indies; no golden minerals are in Malta."

By "the Western Indies," Governor Ferneze was referring to the gold mines of Central and South America.

"To you of Malta, thus says Calymath: The time you took for respite is at hand for the performance of your past promise past, and I have been sent for the tribute money," the Pasha said.

"Pasha, in brief, thou shall have no tribute here," Governor Ferneze said. "Nor shall the heathens live upon the wealth they would get if they sacked our city. First we ourselves will raze to the ground the city walls, lay waste the island, hew the temples down, and, shipping off our goods to Sicily, open an entrance for the devastation-causing sea, whose billows, beating the unresisting banks, shall overflow it with their reflux of water."

"Well, Governor, since thou have broken the league by flat denial of the promised tribute, don't talk about razing your city walls. You shall not need trouble yourselves so far, for Selim Calymath shall come himself, and with brass bullets batter down your towers, and turn proud Malta into a wilderness for these intolerable wrongs of yours. And so, farewell."

"Farewell," Governor Ferneze said.

The Pasha exited.

Governor Ferneze said, "And now, you men of Malta, look about, and let's prepare to welcome Calymath. Close your portcullis, charge your basilisks, and as you profitably — in a worthy cause that can gain you profit — take up arms, so now courageously encounter the Turks in battle, for by this answer of ours the league has been broken, and nothing is to be looked for now but wars, and nothing is to us more welcome than wars."

A portcullis is a strong grating that protects a gateway. A basilisk is a large cannon.

Friar Jacomo and Friar Barnardine talked together.

"Oh, brother, brother, all the nuns are sick, and medicine will not help them," Friar Jacomo said. "They must die."

"The abbess sent for me to be confessed," Friar Barnardine said. "Oh, what a sad confession will there be."

"And so did fair Maria send for me," Friar Jacomo said. "I'll go to her lodging; hereabouts she lies and dwells."

He exited.

Abigail entered the scene.

"What! All dead except only Abigail!" Friar Barnardine said.

"And I shall die, too, for I feel death coming," Abigail replied. "Where is the friar who conversed with me?"

She had previously asked Friar Jacomo to help her get into the nunnery.

"Oh, he has gone to see the other nuns."

"I sent for him, but seeing you have come, you shall be my ghostly father — my spiritual father and confessor. And first know that in this house I lived religiously, chaste, and devout, much sorrowing for my sins. But, before I came …."

"What then?"

"I did offend high heaven so grievously that I am almost desperate and without hope of salvation because of my sins, and one offence torments me more than all the others," Abigail said. "You knew Mathias and Don Lodowick?"

"Yes, what about them?"

"My father contracted me to be married to both of them. First to Don Lodowick: him I never loved. Mathias was the man whom I held dear, and for his sake I became a nun."

"So tell me: How was their end?"

"Both, jealous of my love, were full of malice toward each other, and by my father's cunning and treachery, the gallants were both slain. All the details are set down in full in this paper."

She gave Friar Barnardine a paper.

"Oh, monstrous villainy!" Friar Barnardine said.

"To achieve my peace of mind and my absolution, this I have confessed to thee. Don't reveal what I told you, for if it is revealed, then my father dies."

"Know that confession must not be revealed. The canon law forbids it, and the priest who makes it known, being degraded and deprived of orders first, shall be condemned and excommunicated and so sent to the fire."

Priests could be defrocked and excommunicated for revealing a religious confession. Excommunication is not equivalent to damnation, but it is something taken seriously — especially by priests. Many priests believe that many unrepentant excommunicated sinners end up in the fire of Hell.

"So I have heard," Abigail said. "Please, therefore, keep it secret. Death seizes on my heart. Ah, gentle friar, convert my father so that he may be saved, and witness that I die a Christian."

She died.

Friar Barnardine said, "Aye, and you die a virgin, too; that grieves me most."

He grieved most because no one had had sex with this nun before she died.

Friar Barnardine continued, "But I must go to the Jew, and exclaim against and denounce him and make him stand in fear of me."

Friar Jacomo entered the scene and said, "Oh, brother, all the nuns are dead. Let's bury them."

Friar Barnardine said, "First help me to bury this."

He meant Abigail's body.

He added, "Then go with me, and help me to exclaim against the Jew."

"Why, what has he done?" Friar Jacomo asked.

"A thing that makes me tremble to reveal."

"Has he crucified a child?"

In this culture, rumors circulated that Jews did such things as kidnap and crucify Christian children.

"No, but a worse thing," Friar Barnardine said. "It was told to me in a confession. Thou know it is death if it is revealed.

"Come, let's go."

CHAPTER 4

— 4.1 —

Barabas and Ithamore talked together. Church bells rang for a funeral.

"There is no music compared to a Christian's death knell," Barabas said. "How sweet the bells ring, now the nuns are dead, that sound at other times like tinkers' pans. I was afraid that the poison had not worked, or that, although it worked, it would have done no good, for every year the nuns swell" — he meant, in pregnancy as well as in numbers — "and yet they live. Now all are dead. Not one remains alive."

"That's splendid, master, but do you think that the cause will not be revealed?"

"How can it be revealed, if we two keep the secret?" Barabas asked.

"As far as my part is concerned, you need not fear," Ithamore replied.

"I'd cut thy throat, if I did."

"And with reason, too. But here's a fine, first-class monastery close by us. Good master, let me poison all the monks there."

"Thou shall not need to, for now that the nuns are dead, the monks will die with grief."

"Don't you sorrow for your daughter's death?" Ithamore asked.

"No, but I grieve because she lived so long, a Hebrew born, and she would become a Christian. *Cazzo, diavola*!"

This was Italian for "Cock, she-devil!"

Friar Jacomo and Friar Barnardine entered the scene.

"Look, look, master," Ithamore said. "Here come two religious caterpillars — religious parasites."

"I smelt them before they came," Barabas said.

Ithamore thought, *God-a-mercy, what a nose!*

He then said out loud, "Come, let's leave."

Friar Barnardine said, "Stay, wicked Jew; repent, I say, and stay."

"Thou have offended, so therefore thou must be damned," Friar Jacomo said.

According to Christian theology, sincere repentance leads to forgiveness of sins and eternal life in Heaven.

Barabas whispered to Ithamore, "I fear they know we sent the poisoned broth."

Ithamore whispered back, "And so do I, master; therefore, speak courteously to them."

Friar Barnardine began, "Barabas, thou have —"

Friar Jacomo interrupted, "Aye, that thou have —"

Barabas interrupted to keep them off the topic of the deaths of Mathias and Lodowick: "— true, I have money. What though I have?"

Friar Barnardine began, "Thou are a —"

Friar Jacomo interrupted, "Aye, that thou are a —"

Barabas interrupted, "Why need we talk about all this? I know I am a Jew."

Friar Barnardine began, "Thy daughter —"

Friar Jacomo interrupted, "Aye, thy daughter —"

Barabas interrupted, "Oh, don't speak about her; when I hear about her, then I die with grief."

Friar Barnardine began, "Remember that —"

Friar Jacomo interrupted, "Aye, remember that —"

Barabas interrupted, "I must say that I have been a great usurer."

Friar Barnardine began, "Thou have committed —"

Barabas interrupted, "— fornication? But that was in another country, and besides, the wench is dead."

The excuses "that was in another country, and besides, the wench is dead" are irrelevant.

Friar Barnardine said, "Aye, but Barabas, remember Mathias and Don Lodowick."

"Why, what about them?" Barabas asked.

"I will not say that by a forged challenge they met," Friar Barnardine replied.

He had a religious duty to keep Abigail's confession secret.

Barabas whispered to Ithamore, "She has confessed, and we are both undone."

He said to the two friars, "My bosom intimates —"

He whispered to Ithamore, "But I must dissemble."

He then said out loud, "Oh, holy friars, the burden of my sins lies heavy on my soul, so then please tell me whether or not it is too late now to convert and be a Christian?

"I have been zealous in the Jewish faith, hardhearted to the poor, a covetous wretch, and I would for the sake of money have sold my soul. A hundred for a hundred I have taken — one hundred percent interest — and now for store of wealth I may compare with all the Jews in Malta.

"But what is wealth? I am a Jew, and therefore I am spiritually lost. If penance would serve to atone for my sin, I could afford to whip myself to death —"

Ithamore thought, *And so could I, but penance will not work.*

A fake repentance would not get Ithamore and Barabas into Paradise — you can't scam God.

Barabas continued, "— or to fast, to pray, and to wear a shirt of hair, and on my knees to creep to Jerusalem."

Some penitents mortified the flesh and rejected worldly things by wearing uncomfortable clothing next to their skin. Often, penitents wore hair shirts made of horsehair under their other clothing.

Barabas continued, "Cellars of wine, and lofts full of wheat, warehouses stuffed with spices and with medicines, whole chests of gold in bullion and in coin, besides I know not how much weight in pearls that are orient and lustrous and round have I within my house.

"At Alexandria I have unsold merchandise. Only yesterday two ships sailed from this town: Their voyage will be worth ten thousand crowns. In Florence, Venice, Antwerp, London, Seville, Frankfort, Lubeck, Moscow — where do I not have debts owed to me — and, in most of these cities I have great sums of money lying in the bank.

"All this I'll give to some religious house, as long as I may be baptized, and live therein."

"Oh, good Barabas, come to our house," Friar Jacomo pleaded.

"Oh, no, good Barabas, come to our house," Friar Barnardine said. "And Barabas, you know —"

Barabas said to Friar Barnardine, "I know that I have highly sinned. You shall convert me. You shall have all my wealth."

"Oh, Barabas, the laws of Friar Barnardine's house are strict," Friar Jacomo said.

Barabas said to Friar Jacomo, "I know they are, and I will be with you."

Friar Barnardine said about Friar Jacomo's house, "They wear no shirts, and they go barefoot, too."

He may have meant that the friars of Friar Jacomo's house did not wear regular shirts but instead wore hair shirts. The friars were assuming that Barabas would want to live in a religious house whose rules were relaxed although he had mentioned a moment ago that if penance would serve to atone for his sin, he would do such things as wear a shirt of hair.

Barabas said to Friar Barnardine, "Then it is not for me; and I am resolved that you shall confess me and have all my goods."

"Good Barabas, come to me," Friar Jacomo pleaded.

Barabas said to Friar Barnardine, "You see, I answer him, and yet he stays. Get rid of him and make him go away, and go home with me."

Friar Jacomo said to Barabas, "I'll be with you tonight."

Barabas said to Friar Jacomo, "Come to my house at one o'clock this night."

Friar Barnardine said to Friar Jacomo, "Why, go, get away from here."

"I will not go at your bidding," Friar Jacomo said.

Friar Barnardine said to Friar Jacomo, "You won't? Then I'll make thee, rogue."

"What!" Friar Jacomo said. "Do you dare to call me a rogue?"

Friar Barnardine and Friar Jacomo fought each other.

"Part them, master, part them," Ithamore said.

"This is mere frailty — human weakness," Barabas said. "Brethren, be content. Friar Barnardine, go with Ithamore."

He then whispered to Friar Barnardine, "You know my mind; leave it to me to deal with him. I can handle Friar Jacomo."

Friar Jacomo said to Barabas, "Why does he go to thy house? Let him be gone."

Barabas whispered to Friar Jacomo, "I'll give him something and so stop his mouth."

Ithamore and Friar Barnardine exited.

Barabas said to Friar Jacomo, "I never heard of any man except Friar Barnardine who maligned the order of the Jacobins. But do you think that I believe his words? Why, brother, you converted Abigail, and I am bound in charity to requite it, and so I will. Oh, Jacomo, don't fail, but come to my house tonight."

The word "requite" can mean "charitably repay," but Barabas used the word in the sense of "get revenge for."

"But, Barabas, who shall be your godfathers?" Friar Jacomo asked. "For soon you shall be confessed."

"Indeed, the Turk — Ithamore — shall be one of my godfathers," Barabas said. "But not a word to any of your convent."

Ithamore — a non-Christian Thracian brought up in the part of Arabia that was part of the Turkish Empire — was an unlikely choice for a godfather. Barabas used the word "Turk" to mean "unbeliever in Christianity." This clearly revealed Friar Jacomo's hypocrisy — he did not object to a Turk being one of Barabas' godfathers.

"I promise thee I won't say a word, Barabas," Friar Jacomo said, and then he exited.

Alone, Barabas said to himself, "So, now the fear is past, and I am safe, for Friar Barnardine, who confessed Abigail, is within my house.

"What if I murdered him before Jacomo comes? Now I have such a plot for both their lives as neither the Jews nor the Christians have ever known the like. Jacomo converted my daughter; therefore, he shall die. The other — Barnardine — knows enough to have my life because Abigail confessed to him; therefore, it is not necessary that he should live.

"But aren't both these men 'wise' to suppose that I will leave my house, my goods, and all, in order to fast and to be well whipped? I'll have none of that.

"Now, Friar Barnardine, I come to you. I'll feast you, lodge you, give you fair words, and after that, I and my trusty Turk ... just so. It must and shall be done."

Ithamore entered the scene.

"Ithamore, tell me, is the friar asleep?" Barabas asked.

"Yes, and I don't know what the reason is, but do what I can, he will not strip himself, nor go to bed, but sleeps in his own clothes. I am afraid that he suspects our intentions."

"No; it is a religious observance that the friars follow," Barabas said. "Yet, if he knew our intentions, could he escape?"

"No, none can hear him, no matter how loud he cries."

"Why, that is true," Barabas said. "For that reason, I therefore did place him there. The other chambers open towards the street."

"You loiter, master," Ithamore said. "Why do we delay? Oh, how I long to see him shake his heels as he is strangled."

Barabas said quietly to the sleeping Friar Barnardine, "Come on, sirrah, off with your belt."

He took off Friar Barnardine's belt, which was a piece of rope, and gave it to Ithamore, saying, "Make a handsome noose."

Ithamore made the noose, and handed it to Barabas, who shouted, "Friar, awake!"

Waking up, Friar Barnardine lifted his head, and Barabas slipped the noose around his neck.

"What!" Friar Barnardine said. "Do you intend to strangle me?"

"Yes," Ithamore said, "because you are accustomed to confess the sins of others."

"Don't blame us; instead, blame the proverb 'confess and be hanged,'" Barabas said.

Barabas said to Ithamore, "Pull hard."

"What! Will you have my life?" Friar Barnardine asked.

"Pull hard, I say," Barabas said to Ithamore.

He then said to Friar Barnardine, "You would have had my goods."

"Aye, and our lives, too," Ithamore said to Friar Barnardine.

He then said to Barabas, "Therefore, pull with all your strength."

They pulled, and Friar Barnardine died.

Ithamore said, "It was neatly done, sir. On his neck is no mark from the noose at all."

"Then it is as it should be," Barabas said. "Pick him up."

"Nay, master, take my advice a little," Ithamore replied.

He added, "So, let him lean upon his staff," while he leaned the corpse against a wall and kept it from falling by how he placed the staff.

Barabas placed another staff close by the corpse.

"Excellent!" Ithamore said. "He stands as if he were begging for bacon."

"Who would not think anything but that this friar lived?" Barabas said, and then he asked, "What time of night is it now, sweet Ithamore?"

"Close to one."

"Then Jacomo will not be far from here," Barabas said.

He and Ithamore hid themselves, and then Friar Jacomo entered the scene.

"This is the hour wherein I shall prosper," Friar Jacomo said. "Oh, happy hour in which I shall convert an infidel and bring his gold into our treasury. But quiet! Isn't this Barnardine? It is!

"And understanding that I should come this way, he stands here on purpose, intending to do me some wrong and to intercept my going to the Jew."

He called, "Barnardine!"

He then said, "Will thou not speak? Thou think I don't see thee? Away, I wish thee would go away, and let me go by thee.

"No, will thou not move out of my way? Nay, then I'll force my way.

"And I see that a staff stands ready for the purpose.

"If thou likes that, stop me some other time."

Friar Jacomo grabbed the staff that Barabas had placed by Friar Barnardine's corpse, and he struck Friar Barnardine's corpse. Barnardine's corpse fell, and his head hit the ground hard.

Barabas and Ithamore came out of hiding, and Barabas asked, "Why, how are you now, Jacomo?"

Seeing the corpse on the ground, he said, "Jacomo, what have thou done?"

"Why, I have struck a man who would have struck at me."

"Who is it? Barnardine? Now ... damn! Alas, he is slain."

"Aye, master, he's slain," Ithamore said. "Look how his brains drop out of his nose."

"Good sirs, I have done it," Friar Jacomo said, "but nobody knows it but you two. I may escape."

"So might my serving-man and I hang with you for company," Barabas said.

"No," Ithamore said. "Let us take him to the magistrates."

"Good Barabas, let me go," Friar Jacomo said.

"No, pardon me," Barabas said. "The law must have its course. I must be forced to give in evidence that being importuned by this Barnardine to be a Christian, I shut him out, and there he sat. Now I, to keep my word and give my goods and substance to your house, was up thus early, with intent to go to your friary because you were late in coming to me."

"Bah upon them, master," Ithamore said. "Will you turn Christian, when holy friars turn devils and murder one another?"

"No," Barabas said. "Because of this example of a Christian committing murder, I'll remain a Jew. Heaven bless me! A friar a murderer? When shall you see a Jew commit the like?"

"Why, a Turk could have done no more," Ithamore, who was a Turk, said.

"Tomorrow is the law-court sessions," Barabas said to Friar Jacomo. "You shall go to it and be tried."

He then said, "Come, Ithamore, let's help to take him hence."

"Villains, I am a sacred person," Friar Jacomo said. "I am a friar. Don't touch me."

"The law shall touch you," Barabas said. "We'll but lead you, we will. Alas, I could weep at your calamity."

He said to Ithamore, "Take the staff, too, for that must be shown. Law requires that each particular piece of evidence be known."

The courtesan Bellamira and the thief Pilia-Borza talked together.

Bellamira asked, "Pilia-Borza, did thou meet with Ithamore?"

"I did."

"And did thou deliver my letter?"

"I did."

"And what do thou think? Will he come?"

"I think so. And yet I cannot tell, for, at the reading of the letter he looked like a man of another world — he looked like a ghost."

"Why?"

"That such a base slave as he should be addressed by such a splendid man as I am, from such a beautiful dame as you."

"And what did he say?" Bellamira asked.

"Not a wise word. He only gave me a nod, as if he would say, 'Is it even so? Is this how it stands?' And so I left him driven to a nonplus — a state of bewilderment — at the critical aspect of my terrible countenance."

"Critical aspect" refers to astrology and the sinister influence that some planets and stars have in certain positions. Pilia-Borza had given Ithamore a look that daunted him.

"And where did thou meet him?"

"I saw him upon my own freehold, within forty foot of the gallows, memorizing his neck verse, I take it, while he was looking on at a friar's execution."

Pilia-Borza was a thief and pickpocket, and his freehold — 'his' land — consisted of public places, such as around a gallows, where he could ply his trade.

By what was known as "benefit of clergy," people could escape hanging by proving that they knew Latin — in this culture, mainly priests knew Latin. According to Pilia-Borza, Ithamore was trying to memorize the fifty-first Psalm in Latin in case he ever needed to escape being hung.

In English, this is the first line of Psalm 51: "*Have mercy upon me, O God, according to thy loving-kindness: according to the multitude of thy compassions put away mine iniquities*" (1599 Geneva Bible).

Pilia-Borza continued, "I saluted him — Ithamore — with an old hempen proverb, *hodie tibi, cras mihi*, and so I left him to the mercy of the hangman."

The proverb, which means "Your turn today, my turn tomorrow," is hempen because it is homespun and because it makes a reference to the hempen rope used by the hangman. As a thief, Pilia-Borza would be hung if he were caught. He also was threatening Ithamore with hanging.

Pilia-Borza continued, "But, the exercise — the religious ceremony — being done, see where he comes."

Ithamore arrived on the scene.

He said to himself, "I never knew a man take his death so patiently as this friar. He was ready to leap off before the halter was about his neck."

Apparently, Friar Jacomo was so eager for death — perhaps because he had sincerely repented what he thought was the murder he had committed — that he had not taken advantage of benefit of clergy. Even if he had, he would have been tried in a different court: an ecclesiastical court.

Ithamore continued, "And when the hangman had put on the friar's hempen tippet — the noose — Friar Jacomo made such haste in his prayers, as if he had had another cure to serve — another parish to spiritually serve."

A tippet is a band or scarf of silk or other material worn around a priest's neck.

Ithamore continued, "Well, go whither he will, I'll be none of his followers in haste. And now I think of it, coming to the execution, a fellow met me with a mustache like a raven's wing, and a dagger with a hilt like a long-handled bed-warming pan, and he gave me a letter from one madam Bellamira, saluting me with a low bow as if he had meant to make clean my boots with his lips. The gist was that I should come to her house. I wonder what the reason is. It may be she sees more in me than I can find in myself, for she writes further that she has loved me ever since she saw me. And who would not requite such love? Here's her house, and here she comes, and now I wish I were gone. I am not worthy to look upon her."

Ithamore walked over to Pilia-Borza and Bellamira.

"This is the gentleman you wrote to," Pilia-Borza said to Bellamira.

Ithamore thought, *"Gentleman!" He mocks me. What gentry can be in a poor Turk worth only ten pence? I'll be gone.*

"Isn't he a sweet-faced youth, Pilia-Borza?" Bellamira asked.

Ithamore thought, *Again, a mock: "sweet youth."*

She continued, "Didn't you, sir, bring the sweet youth a letter?"

Pilia-Borza said to Ithamore, "I did, sir, and from this gentlewoman, who, like myself and the rest of the members of the household, stand or fall at your service."

"Though woman's modesty should hold me back, I can hold back no longer," Bellamira said to Ithamore. "Welcome, sweet love."

Ithamore thought, *Now am I clean, or rather foully, out of the way.*

One meaning of the word "clean" is "wholly."

By "out of the way," Ithamore meant "out of my depth." He did not think he was worthy of Bellamira.

He started to leave.

"Going away so soon?" Bellamira asked.

Ithamore thought, *I'll go steal some money from my master to make me handsome.*

He said out loud, "Please, pardon me; I must go see a ship unloaded."

He started to leave again.

"Can thou be so unkind as to leave me thus?" Bellamira asked.

"If only you knew how she loves you, sir!" Pilia-Borza said.

Ithamore replied, "Nay, I don't care how much she loves me."

He did not think that he was worthy of her love — unless he had money to give to her.

He then said, "Sweet Bellamira, I wish I had my master's wealth for thy sake!"

"And you can have it, sir, if you please," Pilia-Borza said.

"If it were above ground, I could and would have it," Ithamore said, "but he hides and buries it as partridges do their eggs, under the earth."

"And isn't it possible to find it out?" Pilia-Borza asked.

"It is by no means possible," Ithamore replied.

Bellamira whispered to Pilia-Borza, "What shall we do with this base villain, then?"

Pilia-Borza whispered back, "Leave it to me; you just speak nice, flattering words to him."

He then said to Ithamore, "But you know some secrets of the Jew, which, if they were revealed, would do him harm."

"Aye, and such as — ah, say no more!" Ithamore said. "I'll make him send me half of the wealth he has, and he'll be glad he escapes so easily, too. Bring me pen and ink! I'll write to him. We'll have money right away."

"Send for a hundred crowns at least," Pilia-Borza said.

"Ten hundred thousand crowns," Ithamore said.

A servant brought him pen and ink and he began to write, saying, "Master Barabas —"

"Don't write so submissively," Pilia-Borza said. "Write threateningly to him."

Ithamore scratched his words out and wrote as he said, "Sirrah Barabas, send me a hundred crowns."

Coming from a servant and directed to a master, the word "sirrah" was disrespectful.

"Put in two hundred at least," Pilia-Borza said.

Writing, Ithamore said, "I order thee to send me three hundred crowns by this bearer, and this shall be your warrant. If you do not — I write no more, but even so you know. You'll suffer the consequences."

The letter was the warrant — it authorized Barabas to give the bearer of the letter the money to carry back to Ithamore.

"Tell him you will confess," Pilia-Borza said.

Writing, Ithamore said, "Otherwise I'll confess all."

He gave the letter to Pilia-Borza and said, "Vanish, and return in a twinkle."

"Leave it to me to deal with him," Pilia-Borza said. "I'll treat him according to his kind."

He meant that he would treat Barabas 1) as a Jew ought to be treated — in this culture, that meant badly, and 2) in accordance with Barabas' character.

Holding the letter, Pilia-Borza exited.

"Hang him, the Jew!" Ithamore said.

"Now, gentle Ithamore, lie in my lap," Bellamira said.

This was sexually suggestive.

He lay in her lap.

She called, "Where are my maids?"

She ordered them, "Provide a running banquet. Bring us a light meal.

"Send to the merchant: Tell him to bring me silks."

She then said, "Shall Ithamore, my love, go in such rags?"

"And tell the jeweler to come hither, too," Ithamore said.

"I have no husband, sweet," Bellamira said. "I'll marry thee."

"Agreed, but we will leave this paltry land and sail from here to Greece, to lovely Greece. I'll be thy Jason, thou my golden fleece."

Jason and his Argonauts succeeded in getting the golden fleece.

Ithamore continued, "Where painted carpets — brightly colored flowers — over the meadows are hurled, and Bacchus' vineyards overspread the world, where woods and forests are dressed in goodly green, I'll be Adonis: thou shall be Venus, Queen of Love."

William Shakespeare's poem *Venus and Adonis* is a tale of unrequited love. Venus loves Adonis, but he wants nothing to do with her. Instead, he wants to go hunting. She has a vision that if he hunts the following day, he will be killed. He does hunt the following day, and a boar kills him. In other tellings of the myth, Adonis returns Venus' love, but he still dies young.

Ithamore continued, "The meadows, the orchards, and the primrose lanes, instead of coarse sedge and reed, bear sugar canes. Thou in those groves, I swear by Dis above, shall live with me, and be my love."

Dis is the god of the Underworld — the Land of the Dead — and so Dis is not above.

"Whither will I not go with gentle Ithamore?" Bellamira said.

Carrying a moneybag, Pilia-Borza returned.

"How is everything now?" Ithamore asked him. "Have thou the gold?"

"Yes."

"But did it come to you freely and easily?" Ithamore asked. "Did the cow let her milk flow freely?"

"While reading the letter, he stared and stamped, and turned aside. I took him by the beard" — this was an insult — "and looked upon him thus" — Pilia-Borza made a threatening face — "and told him it would be best for him to send the money," Pilia-Borza said. "Then he hugged and embraced me."

"Rather out of fear than love," Ithamore said.

"Then, like a Jew, he laughed and jeered, and told me he loved me for your sake, and said what a faithful servant you had been," Pilia-Borza said.

"The more villain he to keep me like this," Ithamore said. "Look at the clothing I am wearing. This is goodly apparel, isn't it?"

Ithamore was wearing poor-quality clothing.

"To conclude, he gave me ten crowns," Pilia-Borza said.

This was either a tip or a bribe.

"Only ten crowns?" Ithamore said. "I'll leave him not worth a grey groat."

A grey groat is a small silver coin.

He said, "Give me a ream of paper. We'll have a kingdom of gold for it."

"Write for five hundred crowns," Pilia-Borza said.

Writing, Ithamore said, "Sirrah Jew, as you love your life, send me five hundred crowns and give the bearer one hundred crowns as a tip."

He then said to Pilia-Borza, "Tell him I must have the money."

"I promise you, your worship shall have it," Pilia-Borza said.

"And, if he should ask why I demand so much, tell him I scorn to write a line demanding anything less than a hundred crowns," Ithamore said.

"You'd make a rich poet, sir," Pilia-Borza said. "I am gone."

He exited.

Ithamore gave the moneybag to Bellamira and said, "Take the money; spend it for my sake."

"It is not thy money, but thyself I value," she said. "Thus Bellamira esteems the gold" — she threw the moneybag to the side: her side, not Ithamore's — "but thus I esteem thee."

She covered his face with kisses.

Ithamore thought, *That kiss again. She runs division of my lips. What an eye she casts on me! It twinkles like a star.*

"Division" is a musical term used to denote a form of variation or ornamentation in which many short notes are rapidly played. Bellamira performed well with her lips; she was a virtuoso when it came to kissing.

"Come, my dear love, let's go in and sleep together," she said.

"Oh, I wish that ten thousand nights were put in one, so that we might sleep seven years together before we wake," Ithamore said.

"Come, amorous wag; first we will banquet, and then we will sleep."

Barabas was reading Ithamore's first letter — the one in which he wanted three hundred crowns in blackmail.

He read out loud, "*Barabas, send me three hundred crowns.*"

He then said, "Plain Barabas? Oh, that wicked courtesan! He was not accustomed to call me 'Barabas.'"

He read out loud, "*Or else I will confess.*"

He then said, "Aye, there it goes — there is the threat. But, if I get him, *coupe de gorge* — I'll cut his throat — for that! He sent a shaggy, tattered, staring lowlife, who when he speaks draws out his grizzled beard and winds it twice or thrice about his ear, whose face has been a grindstone for men's swords. His hands are hacked, some fingers cut quite off, and when he speaks he grunts like a hog, and looks like one who is employed in *catzerie* — roguery — and cross biting, aka wronging a wrongdoer. He is such a rogue as is the husband to a hundred whores, and I by him must send three hundred crowns."

A pimp would pretend to be the husband of a whore in order to blackmail the whore's clients.

Barabas continued, "Well, my hope is, Ithamore will not stay there always. And, when he comes — oh, I wish that he were only here!"

Pilia-Borza entered the scene and said, "Jew, I must have more gold."

"Why?" Barabas asked. "Do thou lack any of thy tally? Is anything missing from the amount you have received?"

"No, but three hundred crowns will not serve his turn," Pilia-Borza replied.

"Not serve his turn, sir?" Barabas said.

"Serve his turn" meant "meet his need." Barabas could guess that Ithamore wanted more money so he could satisfy his sexual desires.

"No, sir, and therefore I must have five hundred crowns more."

Angry, Barabas said, "I'll rather —"

"Oh, speak calm words, sir, and send the money — it is best for you," Pilia-Borza said. "See, there's his letter."

He handed Barabas Ithamore's second letter.

"Might he not as well come in person to me as send you?" Barabas asked. "Please, tell him to come and fetch it himself. The tip that he wrote I should give you — one hundred crowns — you shall have immediately."

"Aye, and the rest, too, or else —"

Barabas thought, *I must do away with — kill — this villain.*

He asked out loud, "Would it please you to dine with me, sir?"

He thought, *If you do, you shall be most heartily poisoned.*

"No, God-a-mercy," Pilia-Borza said. "Shall I have these crowns?"

"I cannot do it," Barabas replied. "I have lost my keys."

"Oh, if that is all, I can pick open your locks."

"Or climb up to my counting-house window?" Barabas said. "You know my meaning?"

Barabas guessed that Pilia-Borza was the person who had earlier climbed up to his window and stolen one of his moneybags.

"I know enough, and therefore don't talk to me about your counting-house. Give me the gold, or know, Jew, it is in my power to get thee hanged."

Barabas thought, *I am betrayed.*

He said out loud, "It is not the five hundred crowns that I esteem. I am not angered at that. This angers me — that he who knows I love him as myself should write in this imperious vein. Why, sir, you know I have no child, and to whom should I leave all I have but to Ithamore?"

"Here's many words, but no crowns," Pilia-Borza said. "The crowns!"

"Commend me to him, sir, most humbly, and commend me to your good mistress, who has not been introduced to me."

"Speak, shall I have the crowns, sir?"

"Sir, here they are," Barabas said, giving him the gold coins.

He thought, *Oh, that I should part with so much gold!*

He said, "Here, take them, fellow, with as good a will" — he thought, *As I would see thee hanged* — "oh, love stops my breath. Never has a man loved a servant as I do Ithamore."

"I know it, sir."

"Please, tell me when, sir, shall I see you at my house?"

"Soon enough to your cost, sir," Pilia-Borza said. "Fare you well."

He exited with the money.

Alone, Barabas said to himself, "Nay, to thine own cost, villain, if thou come.

"Was ever any Jew tormented as I am? To have a shag-rag — shaggy and unkempt — knave to come demand three hundred crowns, and then five hundred crowns!

"Well, I must seek a means to get rid of them all, and immediately; for in his villainy Ithamore will tell all he knows, and I shall die for it.

"I have it. I will in some disguise go see the slave, and I will see how the villain revels with my gold."

— 4.4 —

Bellamira, Ithamore, and Pilia-Borza were drinking in Bellamira's home.

Bellamira said to Ithamore, "I'll offer a toast to thee, love, and therefore you shall drink it off."

"Do thou say that to me? Have at it! And do you hear?" Ithamore said.

He whispered something in her ear, presumably about having at what couples do in bed rather than having at the drinking of wine.

"Ha!" Bellamira said. "Of course, it shall be so."

"On that condition I will drink it up," Ithamore said. "Here's to thee."

He drank part of the wine.

She said, "Nay, I'll have all or none."

She wanted him to drink all the wine in his glass because she wanted to get him drunk. Excessive alcohol consumption increases desire but takes away performance.

"There," Ithamore said after draining his cup of wine. "If thou love me, do not leave a drop."

He wanted her to drain her cup.

"Love thee?" Bellamira said. "Fill three glasses."

"Three and fifty dozen!" Ithamore said. "I'll drink to thee."

"Knavely spoken and like a knight at arms," Pilia-Borza said.

"Hey, *Rivo Castiliano*, a man's a man," Ithamore said.

"*Rivo Castiliano*" means "Castilian stream or river." Ithamore may have been drinking and/or calling for Spanish wine. Or he may have been using the phrase as a nickname for Pilia-Borza.

A proverb stated, "A man's a man, though he have but a hose on his head." The proverb meant that men are equal despite social distinctions such as the kind of hat a man has on his head.

"Now to the Jew," Bellamira said.

"Ha! To the Jew!" Ithamore said. "And send me money — you had better do it."

Pilia-Borza asked, "What would thou do, if he should send thee none?"

"Do nothing, but I know what I know," Ithamore said. "He's a murderer."

"I had not thought he had been so brave a man," Bellamira said.

"You knew Mathias and the Governor's son," Ithamore said. "Barabas and I killed them both, and yet never touched them."

"Oh, splendidly done!" Pilia-Borza said.

"I carried the broth that poisoned the nuns, and he and I, snickle hand too fast, strangled a friar," Ithamore said.

To "snickle" means to "catch with a noose," so by "snickle hand too fast" Ithamore, now drunk, may have meant something such as, "Put the noose on him with a hand too fast to stop."

Or, possibly, he meant, "The snare hand was too fast."

Or, possibly, he meant spoken words: "Snickle! Hand! Too fast!" This passage would then mean something such as, "Put the noose over his head! Deal with him! Make the noose too tight!"

"You two alone murdered the friar?" Bellamira asked.

"We two. And it was never known, nor never shall be, as far as I'm concerned."

Pilia-Borza whispered to Bellamira, "This information shall be delivered by me to the Governor."

She whispered back, "And it is fitting it should be. But first let's have more gold."

She then said, "Come, gentle Ithamore, lie in my lap."

Ithamore sang this song:

"Love me little,

"Love me long;

"Let music rumble,

"Whilst I in thy incony lap do tumble."

The word "incony" means "fine" and "delicate," but Ithamore was punning on "in-cunny." A "cunny" is a "c*nt." To "tumble" is to "have a bout of sex."

Barabas, disguised and carrying a lute, entered the room.

"A French musician!" Bellamira said. "Come, let's hear your skill."

Speaking with a fake French accent, the disguised Barabas said, "Must tune-a my lute for sound, twang, twang, first."

"Will you drink, Frenchman?" Ithamore asked, hiccupping.

He added, "Here's to thee with — hic — a pox on this drunken hiccup!"

"Gramercy, monsieur," the disguised Barabas said. "Many thanks."

"Please, Pilia-Borza, tell the fiddler to give me the nosegay in his hat there," Bellamira said.

A nosegay is a small bouquet of flowers.

Pilia-Borza said to the disguised Barabas, "Sirrah, you must give my mistress your nosegay."

Barabas gave Bellamira the nosegay and said, "I am *à votre commandement*, Madame. I am at your command."

"How sweet, my Ithamore, the flowers smell," Bellamira said.

Ithamore smelled them and said, "Like thy breath, sweetheart; there is no violet like them."

"Yuck! I think they stink like a hollyhock," Pilia-Borza said.

Many people like the scent of a hollyhock.

The disguised Barabas thought, *Good, now I am revenged upon them all. The scent of the nosegay means death; I poisoned it.*

Ithamore ordered, "Play, fiddler, or I'll cut your cat's guts — your lute strings — into chitterlings."

"Chitterlings" are "pork sausages."

"*Pardonnez moi*, pardon me, be no in tune yet," the disguised Barabas said. "So now, now, all is in tune."

"Give him a crown, and pour out more wine for me," Ithamore said.

Pilia-Borza gave the disguised Barabas some money and said, "There's two crowns for thee. Play."

Barabas thought, *How liberally the villain gives me my own gold.*

"I think he fingers very well," Pilia-Borza said.

By "finger," he meant "play the strings."

Barabas thought, *So did you finger well when you stole my gold.*

By "finger," he meant "put your fingers on my gold in order to steal it."

"How swiftly he plays a run of notes," Pilia-Borza said.

The disguised Barabas thought, *You ran swifter when you threw my gold out of my window.*

"Musician, have you been in Malta long?" Bellamira asked.

"Two, three, four month, madam," the disguised Barabas said, using incorrect grammar.

"Do you know a Jew named Barabas?" Ithamore asked.

"Very mush, monsieur, you no be his man?" the disguised Barabas asked.

His fake French accent made "mush" out of "much."

By "man," he meant "man-servant."

"His man?" Pilia-Borza asked.

Referring to Barabas, Ithamore said, "I scorn the peasant; tell him so."

The disguised Barabas thought, *He knows it already.*

"It is a strange thing about that Jew," Ithamore said. "He lives on pickled grasshoppers and seasoned mushrooms."

Pickled grasshoppers and seasoned mushrooms are inexpensive food.

The disguised Barabas thought, *What a slave is this! Governor Ferneze does not eat as well as I do.*

"He has never put on a clean shirt since he was circumcised," Ithamore said.

The disguised Barabas thought, *Oh, rascal! I change my clothing twice a day.*

"The hat he wears — it is the one Judas left under the elder tree when he hanged himself," Ithamore said.

The disguised Barabas thought, *It was sent to me as a present by the Great Khan.*

"A masty slave he is," Pilia-Borza said.

The adjective "masty" means "fattened on mast, aka food for pigs."

Barabas started to leave.

"Where are you going now, fiddler?" Pilia-Borza asked.

"*Pardonnez moi*, pardon me, monsieur," the disguised Barabas said. "Me be no well."

He exited.

"Farewell, fiddler," Pilia-Borza said.

He said to Ithamore, "One more letter to the Jew."

"Please, sweet love, one more, and write it sharply worded," Bellamira said to Ithamore.

"No, I'll send by word of mouth now," Ithamore replied.

He said to Pilia-Borza, "Order him to deliver to thee a thousand crowns. He will give it to thee if you say that the nuns loved rice or that Friar Barnardine slept in his own clothes. Either of them will do it."

"Leave it to me to persuade him to give me the money, now that I know the meaning behind the words you said," Pilia-Borza said.

"The meaning has a meaning," Ithamore said, attempting to appear deep and mysterious and forgetting that he had already talked about these murders.

He said to Bellamira, "Come, let's go in. To ruin a Jew is charity, and not sin."

CHAPTER 5
— 5.1 —

Governor Ferneze, some Knights of Malta, Martin del Bosco, and some officers were meeting to discuss military defense and strategy.

"Now, gentlemen, take yourselves to your arms, and see that Malta is well fortified," Governor Ferneze said. "And it behooves you to be resolute, for Calymath, having waited near here so long, will win the town or die before the walls."

"And die he shall, for we will never yield," the first Knight of Malta said.

Bellamira and Pilia-Borza entered the scene.

"Oh, take us to the Governor," Bellamira said.

"Take her away!" Governor Ferneze said. "She is a courtesan."

"Whatever I am, yet, Governor, hear me speak," Bellamira said. "I bring thee news concerning by whom thy son was slain. Mathias did not do it: It was the Jew."

"The Jew, besides the slaughter of these gentlemen, poisoned his own daughter and the nuns, strangled a friar, and committed I know not what other evil besides," Pilia-Borza said.

"Had we but proof of this —" Governor Ferneze began.

Bellamira interrupted, "— we have strong proof, my lord. His serving-man's now at my lodging. He was the Jew's agent; he'll confess it all."

"Go fetch him immediately," Governor Ferneze said. "I always feared that Jew."

Some officers left and quickly brought in Barabas and Ithamore.

"I'll go alone," Barabas said to the officers. "Dogs, do not drag me thus."

"Nor me either," Ithamore said. "I cannot outrun you, constable."

He grabbed his midsection and said, "Oh, my belly!"

He was feeling the effects of Barabas' poison.

Barabas thought, *One dram of powder more had made everything safe and secure for me. What a damned slave I was not to use more poison!*

Governor Ferneze ordered, "Make fires! Heat irons! Let the rack be fetched!"

He was going to torture a confession out of Barabas and Ithamore.

"Nay, wait, my lord," the first Knight of Malta said. "It may be the case that he will confess."

"Confess?" Barabas said. "What do you mean, lords? Who should confess?"

"Thou and thy Turk," Governor Ferneze said. "It was you who slew my son."

Ithamore said, "I am guilty, my lord, I confess; your son and Mathias were both betrothed to Abigail. Barabas forged a counterfeit challenge."

"Who carried that challenge?" Barabas asked.

"I carried it, I confess," Ithamore answered. "But who wrote it? Indeed, even that man who strangled Friar Barnardine, poisoned the nuns, and with them poisoned his own daughter."

"Take him away!" Governor Ferneze ordered. "His sight is death to me."

Barabas said, "Away with me! For what? You men of Malta, hear me speak. She" — he pointed to Bellamira — "is a courtesan, and he" — he pointed to Pilia-Borza — "is a thief, and he" — he pointed to Ithamore — "is my slave. Let me have law, for none of this can be prejudicial against my life."

In this society, slave-owners had rights, such as the right to not have to legally respond to many accusations made against the slave-owner by his slaves and the slave's companions. Barabas wanted no trial.

"Once more, away with him!" Governor Ferneze said.

He then said to Barabas, "You shall have law."

In this society, Jews were second-class people. The "law" that Governor Ferneze meant was "punishment to the full extent that the law would allow."

"Devils, do your worst," Barabas said. "I live in spite of you. As these have spoken, so be it charged to their souls! May their souls suffer the torment that their words make them deserve!"

He thought, *I hope the poisoned flowers will do their work soon.*

Some officers led away Barabas, Ithamore, Bellamira, and Pilia-Borza.

Katherine, Mathias' mother, entered the scene and said, "Was my Mathias murdered by the Jew? Ferneze, it was thy son who murdered him."

"Be patient, gentle madam," Governor Ferneze said. "The murderer is the Jew. He forged the challenge that dared your son to fight a duel. That forged challenge made them fight."

"Where is the Jew?" Katherine asked. "Where is that murderer?"

"He is in prison until the law has passed sentence on him," Governor Ferneze said.

The first officer returned and said, "My lord, the courtesan and her man are dead. So are the Turk and Barabas the Jew."

"Dead?" Governor Ferneze asked.

"Dead, my lord," the first officer said, "and here they bring the Jew's body."

"This sudden death of his is very strange," Martin del Bosco said.

Some officers returned, carrying Barabas.

"Don't wonder at it, sir," Governor Ferneze said. "The heavens are just. Their deaths were like their lives; so then don't think about them. Since they are dead, let them be buried. As for the Jew's body, throw that over the walls to be a prey for vultures and wild beasts."

They threw Barabas over the wall.

"Good," Governor Ferneze said, and then he ordered, "Now go away and fortify the town."

Everyone exited.

The wall was low, and Barabas soon stood up. He had drunk a potion to make him sleep and appear to be dead.

Now outside the walls of the town, Barabas said, "All alone? Blessings on you, sleep-inducing drink! I'll be revenged on this accursed town, for by my means Calymath shall enter in the city. I'll help to slay Malta's citizens' children and their wives. I'll set on fire the churches, pull their houses down, take back my goods, too, and seize my lands. I hope to see Governor Ferneze made a slave, and, rowing in a galley, whipped to death."

Selim Calymath arrived, accompanied by some Pashas and Turks.

Seeing Barabas, Selim Calymath asked, "Whom have we there? A spy?"

"Yes, my good lord, one who can spy a place where you may enter and take the town by surprise," Barabas said. "My name is Barabas; I am a Jew."

"Are thou that Jew whose goods we heard were sold for tribute money?" Selim Calymath asked.

"I am the very same, my lord," Barabas said. "And since that time they have hired a slave, my serving-man, to accuse me of a thousand villainies. I was imprisoned, but I escaped their hands."

"Did you break out of prison?"

"No, no. I drank a sleep-inducing potion made of poppy and cold mandrake juice, and as I slept, it seems they thought I was dead and threw me over the walls. In that way — or how else? — I the Jew am here and remain at your command."

"It was splendidly done. But tell me, Barabas, can thou, as thou report, make Malta ours?"

"Fear not, my lord," Barabas said, "for here against the sluice — the sliding-gate that controls the passage of sewage from the city — the rock is hollow. It was dug on purpose to make a passage for the running streams and public sewers of the city.

"Now, while you assault the walls, I'll lead five hundred soldiers through the vault and rise with them in the middle of the town, open the gates for you to enter in, and by this means the city will be your own."

"If this is true, I'll make thee Governor."

"And if it is not true, then let me die."

"You have passed sentence on yourself," Selim Calymath said. "We will carry out that sentence if what you say is not true. Carry out the assault quickly."

The two sides fought the battle. Barabas led 500 Turks, and they and Selim Calymath took Governor Ferneze and the Knights of Malta prisoners. Now, they stood together. With them were some Pashas and some well-trained Turkish infantrymen who were known as Janizaries.

"Now humble your pride, you captive Christians," Selim Calymath said, "and kneel for mercy to your conquering foe. Now where's the hope you had of help from haughty Spain?

"Ferneze, speak. Had it not been much better to have kept thy promise than to be thus taken by surprise?"

"What should I say?" Governor Ferneze said. "We are captives, and we must yield."

Selim Calymath said, "Aye, villains, you must yield, and under Turkish yokes you shall groan and bear the burden of our anger.

"And, Barabas, as formerly we promised thee, for thy desert we make thee Governor. Treat these prisoners as you wish."

"Thanks, my lord," Barabas replied.

"Oh, fatal day!" Governor Ferneze said. "To fall into the hands of such a traitor and unhallowed Jew! What greater misery could heaven inflict?"

Selim Calymath said, "This is our command."

He added, "Barabas, we give, to guard thy person, these our Janizaries. Treat them well, as we have treated thee.

"And now, brave Pashas, come. We'll walk about the ruined town, and see the destruction we made.

"Farewell, brave Jew. Farewell, great Barabas."

"May all good fortune follow Calymath," Barabas said.

Selim Calymath and the Pashas exited.

Barabas said, "And now, as the first step to ensuring our safety, take the Governor and these Captains, his companions and confederates, to prison."

"Oh, villain, heaven will be revenged on thee," Governor Ferneze said.

"Away!" Barabas said. "No more! Let him not trouble me."

Everyone except Barabas exited.

Alone, Barabas said to himself, "Thus have thou — me — gotten by thy cunning policy no humble position, no small authority. I now am Governor of Malta, true, but Malta hates me, and, because the Maltese hate me my life's in danger. And what good does it do thee, poor Barabas, to be the Governor, seeing that thy life shall be at their command? Leaders can be assassinated.

"No, Barabas, this must be looked into and dealt with, and since by doing wrong thou got authority, bravely keep thy authority by making use of firm and cunning policy. At least, don't lose it without first making a profit, for he who lives in authority, and neither gets himself friends nor fills his moneybags, lives like the ass that Aesop spoke of: The ass labors with a load of bread and wine and when the load is taken off, the ass snaps at and feeds on thistle tops. Asses, who eat thistle, labor for the advantage of their masters, who drink wine and eat bread.

"But Barabas will be more circumspect.

"Begin quickly; seize Lady Opportunity by the forelock because the back of her head is bald. Don't let thine opportunity slip past thee, for fear that too late thou will seek for much, but cannot acquire it."

He then called, "Within here!"

Governor Ferneze, under guard, entered the room.

"My lord?" Governor Ferneze asked.

Barabas thought, *Aye, he said, "Lord"! Thus slaves will learn.*

He said, "Now, Governor, stand to the side there."

He ordered the guard, "Wait outside."

The guard exited.

Barabas said to Governor Ferneze, "This is the reason that I sent for thee. Thou see thy life and Malta's happiness are at my disposal, and Barabas at his discretion may do with both as he wishes. Now tell me, Governor, and plainly, too, what do thou think shall become of Malta's happiness and thee?"

"This, Barabas: Since things are in thy power, I see no reason to expect anything but Malta's ruin, nor do I hope of anything from thee but extreme cruelty," Governor Ferneze said. "Neither do I fear death, nor will I flatter thee."

"Governor, speak good words — don't be so furious. My taking your life will in no way help me. You still live, and you shall live as far as I am concerned, and as for Malta's ruin, don't you think it would be a stupid policy for Barabas to dispossess himself of such a place? For since, as once you said, within this isle, in Malta here, I have gotten my goods and acquired my wealth, and in this city I still have had success, and now at length I am grown to be your Governor, you yourselves shall see it shall not be forgotten. For, as a friend who is not recognized except when Malta is in distress, I'll raise up and relieve Malta, which is now without hope of help."

"Will Barabas recapture Malta?" Governor Ferneze asked. "Will Barabas be good to Christians?"

"What will thou give me, Governor Ferneze, to procure a dissolution of the enslaving bands wherein the Turk has yoked your land and you?

"What will you give me if I deliver to you the life of Calymath, surprise his men, and in a building outside of the city shut his soldiers until I have consumed them all with fire?

"What will you give the man who achieves this?"

"Do but bring this to pass that which thou propose, deal truly with us as thou intimate you will, and I will send among the citizens and by my letters secretly procure great sums of money for thy recompense. Nay, more, do this, and continue still to live as the Governor of Malta."

"Nay, do thou this, Ferneze, and be free," Barabas said. "Governor, I set thee free. Live with me. Go walk about the city; see thy friends. Tush, send not letters to them: Go thyself, and let me see what money thou can gather.

"Here is my hand promising that I'll set Malta free" — he held out his hand — "and thus we devise a plan: To a ceremonial feast I will invite young Selim Calymath. There thou will be present only to perform one stratagem that I'll impart to thee, wherein no danger shall happen to thy life, and I will promise that Malta will be free forever."

"Here is my hand," Governor Ferneze said.

They shook hands.

He continued, "Believe me, Barabas, I will be there, and do as thou desire. When is the time you will put your plan in action?"

"Governor, right away," Barabas said, "for Selim Calymath, when he has viewed the town, will take his leave and sail toward the great Emperor of Turkey in the center of the Ottoman Empire."

"Then, Barabas, I will set about raising this money," Governor Ferneze said, "and I will bring it with me to thee in the evening."

"Do so, but fail not," Barabas said. "Now farewell, Ferneze."

Governor Ferneze exited.

Alone, Barabas said to himself, "And thus far briskly and successfully goes the business. Thus, loving neither side, I will live with both sides, making a profit from my cunning and trickery.

"And he from whom my greatest advantage comes shall be my friend. This is the life we Jews are accustomed to lead — and with reason, too, for Christians do the same.

"Well, now about effecting this device. First to ambush great Selim's soldiers, and then to make provision for the feast, so that at one instant all things may be done.

"My cunning plan detests detection that can lead to prevention. To what outcome my secret purpose drives I alone know — and they shall witness it with their lives. In other words, they will know that my plot succeeded when they die."

Selim Calymath and some Pashas talked together.

"Thus have we viewed the city, seen the plundering of the city, and caused the ruins to be new-repaired, where with the shot of our bombards and basilisks — two types of cannon — we rent in sunder at our entry two lofty turrets that command the town.

"And now I see the situation, and how secure this conquered island stands, surrounded by the Mediterranean Sea, strongly countermured — double-walled — with other petty isles and, toward Calabria in Italy, defended by Sicily, where Syracusian Dionysius reigned, I marvel that it could be conquered thus easily."

A messenger arrived and said, "From Barabas, Malta's Governor, I bring a message to mighty Calymath. Hearing his sovereign was bound for sea, to sail to Turkey, to the great Ottoman — the Emperor of Turkey — he humbly would entreat your majesty to come and see his homely citadel and banquet with him before thou leave the isle."

"To banquet with him in his citadel?" Selim Calymath said. "I am afraid, messenger, that to feast my train of soldiers within a town by war so lately pillaged will be too costly and too troublesome. Yet I would gladly visit Barabas, for Barabas has deserved well of us."

The messenger replied, "Selim, as for that, thus says the Governor: He says that he has in his possession a pearl so big, so precious, and so lustrous that if it is valued fairly and impartially, its price will serve to entertain Selim and all his soldiers for a month. Therefore, he humbly would entreat your highness not to depart until he has feasted you."

"I cannot feast my men inside Malta's walls," Selim Calymath said, "unless he places his tables in the streets."

"Know, Selim, that there is a monastery that stands as a house outside of the town," the messenger said. "There Barabas will serve a banquet to them, but to thee at his home, with all thy Pashas and brave followers."

"Well, tell Governor Barabas we grant his suit," Selim Calymath said. "We'll feast with him this summer evening."

"I shall tell him, my lord," the messenger said.

The messenger exited.

"And now, bold Pashas, let us go to our tents, and consider how we may prepare ourselves best to celebrate our Governor's great feast," Selim Calymath said.

Governor Ferneze, some Knights of Malta, and Martin del Bosco talked together.

"In this, my countrymen, take my advice," Governor Ferneze said. "Take special care that no man ventures forth until you hear a culverin discharged by the man who bears the linstock, kindled thus."

A culverin is a long-barreled cannon; a linstock is a staff with a forked head that holds a lighted match that is used to fire the cannon.

He continued, "Then issue out and come to rescue me, for perhaps I shall be in distress. Even if I am not in distress, you will still be freed from this Turkish servitude."

"Rather than thus to live as Turkish slaves," the first Knight of Malta said, "what will we not risk?"

"Onward, then," Governor Ferneze said. "Take your positions."

"Farewell, honored Governor," the Knights of Malta said.

— 5.5 —

On a balcony in his home, Barabas was very busy with a hammer, as were some carpenters.

Barabas asked, "How stand the cords? How hang these hinges? Are they secure? Are all the cranes and pulleys sure?"

"All are secure," the first carpenter said.

"Leave nothing loose; build everything according to my specifications," Barabas said.

He looked over their work and said, "Why, now I see that you have skill indeed."

He gave them money and said, "There, carpenters, divide that gold among yourselves. Go, swill in bowls of sack — Spanish white wine — and muscatel. Go down to the cellar; taste all of my wines."

"We shall, my lord, and thank you," the first carpenter said.

The carpenters left.

Alone, Barabas said after them, "And if you like them, drink your fill and die! For, as long as I continue to live, I don't care if all the rest of the world perishes!"

He may have poisoned the wine in order to dispose of witnesses, or he may have meant for them to die whenever they would — he didn't care.

He added, "Now, Selim Calymath, return to me word that thou will come, and I am satisfied."

The messenger arrived.

"Now, sirrah," Barabas said. "Will Selim Calymath come?"

"He will," the messenger replied, "and he has commanded all his men to come ashore and march through Malta's streets, so that thou may feast them in thy citadel."

"Then now are all things as my wish would have them," Barabas said. "There lacks nothing but Governor Ferneze's money, and look, he is bringing it."

Governor Ferneze arrived, carrying moneybags.

Barabas asked, "Now, Governor, what is the sum you have collected for me?"

Governor Ferneze replied, "With free consent, a hundred thousand pounds."

"Pounds, say thou, Governor?" Barabas said. "Well, since it is no more, I'll satisfy myself with that."

A pound is worth much more than a crown.

Governor Ferneze offered Barabas the moneybags, but Barabas said, "Nay, keep it for now, for if I don't keep my promise, don't trust me.

"And, Governor, now learn my plot: First, as for Selim Calymath's army, they have been sent ahead and have entered the monastery, underneath which in several places are light cannon pitched; bombards, aka large cannon; and whole barrels full of gunpowder that on the sudden shall shatter the monastery and batter all the stones about their ears, from which none can possibly escape alive.

"Now, as for Selim Calymath and his consorts, here I have made a delightful balcony. The floor of the balcony, when this cable is cut" — he pointed to the cable, which was near Governor Ferneze — "will fall to pieces, so that what is on the floor will sink into a deep pit past recovery."

From the balcony, Barabas tossed near Governor Ferneze a sheathed knife and said, "Here, hold that knife. And when thou see he comes and with his Pashas shall be cheerfully set down at the table, a signal-gun shall be shot off from the tower, to give thee knowledge when to cut the cord and fire off the explosives under the house. Tell me, won't this be splendid?"

"Oh, excellent!" Governor Ferneze said. "Here, wait, Barabas."

He again offered Barabas the moneybags, saying, "I trust thy word; take what I promised thee."

"No, Governor," Barabas said. "I'll satisfy thee first. Thou shall not live in doubt of anything. Stand close by, hidden, for here they come."

Governor Ferneze hid himself.

Barabas said to you, the readers, "Why, isn't this a kingly kind of trade, to purchase towns by treachery, and sell them by deceit? Now tell me, worldlings, whether greater falsehood ever has been done underneath the sun?"

"Worldlings" are people who are devoted to their own self-advancement. Barabas was asking you worldlings to admire his Machiavellian cunning and deceit.

Selim Calymath and the Pashas entered the scene.

"Come, my companion Pashas," Selim Calymath said. "Look, please, at how busy Barabas is there above to entertain us on his balcony. Let us greet him."

He called, "May God save thee, Barabas!"

"Welcome, great Calymath," Barabas replied.

Governor Ferneze thought, *How that slave Barabas jeers at Selim Calymath!*

"Will it please thee, mighty Selim Calymath, to ascend our plain, simple stairs?"

"Aye, Barabas," Selim Calymath said. "Come, Pashas, ascend the stairs."

Governor Ferneze stepped out from his hiding place and said, "Stop, Calymath! For I will show thee greater courtesy than Barabas would have afforded thee."

A Knight of Malta, one of Governor Ferneze's loyal followers, yelled, "Sound a trumpet charge there!"

The trumpet charge sounded, Governor Ferneze cut the cable, and Barabas fell through a trap door into a cauldron with a fire lit under it.

Some depictions of Hell show greedy sinners being boiled alive.

In addition, the signal-gun fired in the tower, and the explosives went off under the monastery.

The Knights of Malta and Martin del Bosco entered the scene.

"What is this!" Selim Calymath said. "What is the meaning of this?"

"Help, help me, Christians, help," Barabas screamed in the steaming water.

"Look, Calymath," Governor Ferneze said. "This was devised for thee. Barabas wanted to boil you to death."

"Treason, treason!" Selim Calymath said. "Pashas, flee!"

"No, Selim, do not flee," Governor Ferneze said. "See Barabas die first, and flee then if thou can."

"Oh, help me, Selim!" Barabas screamed. "Help me, Christians! Governor, why do you all stand so pitiless?"

"Should I in pity of thy lamentations or thee, accursed Barabas, base Jew, relent?" Governor Ferneze said. "No, I'll see thy treachery thus repaid, but I wish thou had behaved otherwise."

"You will not help me, then?" Barabas asked.

"No, villain, no," Governor Ferneze answered.

"And, villains, know you cannot help me now," Barabas said. "I know that I am going to die. So then, Barabas, breathe forth the last breaths that fate allows you, and in the fury of thy torments strive to end thy life with fortitude.

"Know, Governor, that it was I who slew thy son. I wrote the challenge that made them meet.

"Know, Calymath, I planned thy overthrow, and if I had only escaped this stratagem, I would have brought destruction on you all, damned Christian dogs and Turkish infidels!

"But now the extreme intensity of heat begins to torment me with intolerable pangs."

The cauldron boiled.

Barabas screamed, "Die, life! Fly, soul! Tongue, curse thy fill, and die!"

He died.

"Tell me, you Christians, what does this mean?" Selim Calymath asked.

"This plot Barabas laid to have entrapped thy life," Governor Ferneze said. "Now, Selim, note the unhallowed deeds of Jews. Thus he determined to have treated thee, but I have rather chosen to save thy life."

"Was this the banquet he prepared for us?" Selim Calymath asked.

He said to the Pashas, "Let's go away from here, lest further evil be intended."

"Nay, Selim, stay," Governor Ferneze said, "for, since we have thee here, we will not let thee part so suddenly. Besides, if we should let thee go, it would make no difference, for with thy galleys thou could not go away from here without different men to rig and garrison them."

"Tush, Governor, don't worry about that," Selim Calymath said. "My men are all aboard, and they await my coming there at this time."

This was a bluff.

"Why, didn't thou hear the trumpet sound a charge?" Governor Ferneze asked.

"Yes, what of that?"

"Why, then the monastery was fired on by cannon and blown up, and all thy soldiers were massacred."

"Oh, monstrous treason!"

"A Jew's courtesy," Governor Ferneze said. "For he who by treason brought about our downfall by treason has delivered thee to us. Know, therefore, that until thy father has made good the ruins done to Malta and to us, thou cannot depart. For Malta shall be freed, or Selim shall never return to his father, the Emperor of Turkey."

"Instead, Christians, let me go to Turkey, in person there to mediate your peace," Selim Calymath said. "To keep me here will bring no advantage to you."

"Accept this, Selim Calymath," Governor Ferneze said. "Here thou must stay, and live in Malta as our prisoner, for even if all the world were to come to rescue thee, so will we guard ourselves now, that sooner shall they drink the ocean dry than conquer Malta or endanger us.

"So let us march away, and let due praise be given neither to Fate nor Fortune, but to Heaven."

APPENDIX A: NOTES
Cast of Characters: Barabas

This is Matthew 27:15-26 (1599 Geneva Bible):

15 Now at the feast the governor was wont to deliver unto the people a prisoner whom they would.

16 And they had then a notable prisoner called Barabbas.

17 When they were then gathered together, Pilate said unto them, Whether will ye that I let loose unto you Barabbas, or Jesus which is called Christ?

18 (For he knew well, that for envy they had delivered him.

19 Also when he was set down upon the judgment seat, his wife sent to him, saying, Have thou nothing to do with that just man: for I have suffered many things this day in a dream by reason of him.)

20 But the chief Priests and the elders had persuaded the people that they should ask Barabbas, and should destroy Jesus.

21 Then the governor answered, and said unto them, Whether of the twain will ye that I let loose unto you? And they said, Barabbas.

22 Pilate said unto them, What shall I do then with Jesus, which is called Christ? They all said to him, Let him be crucified.

23 Then said the governor, But what evil hath he done? Then they cried the more, saying, Let him be crucified.

24 When Pilate saw that he availed nothing, but that more tumult was made, he took water and washed his hands before the multitude, saying, I am innocent of the blood of this just man: look you to it.

25 Then answered all the people, and said, His blood be on us, and on our children.

26 Thus let he Barabbas loose unto them, and scourged Jesus, and delivered him to be crucified.

Mark 15:7 states, "*Then there was one named Barabbas, which was bound with his fellows, that had made insurrection, who in the insurrection had committed murder*" (1599 Geneva Bible).

Luke 23:18-19 (1599 Geneva Bible) states this:

18 Then all the multitude cried at once, saying, Away with him, and deliver unto us Barabbas:

19 Which for a certain insurrection made in the city, and murder, was cast in prison.

John 18:40 states, "*Then cried they all again, saying, Not him, but Barabbas: now this Barabbas was a murderer*" (1599 Geneva Bible).

John 18:40 states, "*Then cried they all again, saying, Not this man, but Barabbas. Now Barabbas was a robber*" (King James Bible).

Recommended Reading: "Why was Barabbas in prison?[1]"__Biblical Hermeneutics Beta[2].

<https://tinyurl.com/ydg5mxmd>.

---

1.   https://hermeneutics.stackexchange.com/questions/16/why-was-barabbas-in-prison

2.   https://hermeneutics.stackexchange.com/

The Prologue

The story about the cranes is retold from this book:

Barnstone, Willis, translator. *Greek Lyric Poetry*. New York: Schocken Books, 1967. Page 113.

Here is another story about birds revealing a murder:

Bessus, it is said, killed his father, and escaped detection for a long time. But at length, going to supper among strangers, he shook down a swallow's nest with his spear, and killed the young birds; and when those present asked, as was natural, what had provoked him to do so strange a thing, he said, "Do they not, even of old, bear false witness against me, and cry out that I killed my father?" Those who heard him, marvelling at what he said, told the king, and, on investigation, Bessus suffered due punishment.

Source: *Plutarch on the Delay of the Divine Justice*. Andrew P. Peabody, translator. Boston: Little, Brown, and Company, 1885.

The Plutarch book's Latin title is *De Sera Numinis Vindica*. It is part of Book 7 of the 14 books of Plutarch's *Moralia*.

— 1.2 —

Barabas would agree with Machiavelli's observation that "above all things [the prince] must keep his hands off the property of others, because men more quickly forget the death of their father than the loss of their patrimony."

The Machiavelli quotation comes from Chapter 17: "Concerning Cruelty And Clemency, And Whether It Is Better To Be Loved Than Feared" of *The Prince*. Here is the full paragraph:

Nevertheless a prince ought to inspire fear in such a way that, if he does not win love, he avoids hatred; because he can endure very well being feared whilst he is not hated, which will always be as long as he abstains from the property of his citizens and subjects and from their women. But when it is necessary for him to proceed against the life of someone, he must do it on proper justification and for manifest cause, but above all things he must keep his hands off the property of others, because men more quickly forget the death of their father than the loss of their patrimony. Besides, pretexts for taking away the property are never wanting; for he who has once begun to live by robbery will always find pretexts for seizing what belongs to others; but reasons for taking life, on the contrary, are more difficult to find and sooner lapse. But when a prince is with his army, and has under control a multitude of soldiers, then it is quite necessary for him to disregard the reputation of cruelty, for without it he would never hold his army united or disposed to its duties.

Source: Machiavelli, N. *The Prince*. Translated by W. K. Marriott. 1908. <https://www.constitution.org/mac/prince17.htm>

— 1.2 —

Cicero wrote "summum ius, summa iniuria" *in* De Officiis *I.x.33. Walter Miller translated this as "More law, less justice."*

Walter Miller wrote this:

Injustice often arises also through chicanery, that is, through an over-subtle and even fraudulent construction of the law. This it is that gave rise to the now familiar saw, "More law, less justice."

Source: An excerpt from Cicero, *De Officiis* I.x.33.

Source: M. Tullius Cicero. *De Officiis*. With An English Translation. Walter Miller, translator. Cambridge. Harvard University Press; Cambridge, Mass., London, England, 1913.

— 2.1 —

In Spanish, Barabas said this:

"*Birn para todos mi ganado no er.*"

The above are the words that appear in the original quarto; however, *birn* may be *bueno* or *bien*, and *er* may be *era* or *es*.

This could mean three sentences:

Sentence #1:

Bueno para todos mi ganado no era.

This can be translated in various ways:

1. "My flock or wealth, good for everyone else, was of no benefit to me." — David Bevington.

Source: Marlowe, Christopher. *The Jew of Malta*. David Bevington, ed. Manchester and New York: Manchester University Press, 1997. This is the Revels Student edition, which is based on the Revels Plays edition.

2. "My wealth does not avail me in every emergency." — Spencer, from a note on p. 35 in the New Mermaids edition.

Source: Marlowe, Christopher. *The Jew of Malta*. T. W. Craik, editor. New York: Hill and Wang, 1967.

3. "It may be freely rendered 'My flock (i.e., wealth) is not good for all.'" — H.S. Bennett.

Source: Marlowe, Christopher. *The Jew of Malta*. H.S. Bennett, editor. New York: Gordian Press, 1966.

4. "My gain was not good for everybody." — Frank Romany and Robert Lindsey.

Source: Marlowe, Christopher. *The Complete Plays*. Frank Romany and Robert Lindsey, editors. London: Penguin Books, 2003.

5. "My gain is not good for everybody." — Mark Thornton Burnett.

Source: Marlowe, Christopher. *The Complete Plays*. Mark Thornton Burnett, editor. London and Vermont: Everyman, 1999.

6. "My flock (i.e. wealth), good for everyone else, is no good to me." — David Bevington and Eric Rasmussen.

Source: Marlowe, Christopher. *Doctor Faustus and Other Plays*. David Bevington and Eric Rasmussen, editors. Oxford and New York: Oxford University Press, 2008.

Sentence #2:

Bien para todos mi ganado no es.

This can be translated in various ways:

1. "What's good for everyone else is of no benefit to me." — Richard W. Van Fossen.

Source: Marlowe, Christopher. *The Jew of Malta*. Richard W. Van Fossen, editor. Lincoln, Nebraska: University of Nebraska Press, 1964.

2. "My gain is not good for everyone." — N. W. Bawcutt.

N. W. Bawcutt writes that this has "the implication 'I don't want to hand over the money I have gained to everyone'" (p. 100).

Source: Marlowe, Christopher. *The Jew of Malta*. N. W. Bawcutt, editor. Manchester, England and Baltimore, Maryland: Manchester University Press and The Johns Hopkins University Press, 1978.

3. "My gain is not good for everybody — i.e. I don't want to hand over the money I gained to everybody" — David Bevington.

Source: Marlowe, Christopher. *The Jew of Malta*. David Bevington, editor. Manchester and New York: Manchester University Press, 1997. This is the Revels Student edition, which is based on the Revels Plays edition.

4. "My wealth is not good for everybody." — Stephen J. Lynch.

Source: Marlowe, Christopher. *The Jew of Malta*. Stephen J. Lynch, editor. Indianapolis and Cambridge: Hackett Publishing Company, Inc., 2009.

Sentence #3:

Bien, para todos mi ganado no es.

This can be translated in this way:

"Well, my money isn't for everybody." — N.W. Bawcutt, who in a note gives credit to Dr. D.W. Lomax for the idea of putting a comma after "*Bien*."

Source: Marlowe, Christopher. *The Jew of Malta*. N. W. Bawcutt, editor. Manchester, England and Baltimore, Maryland: Manchester University Press and The Johns Hopkins University Press, 1978.

"If it were above ground, I could and would have it," Ithamore said, *"but he hides and buries it as partridges do their eggs, under the earth."*

This mistaken idea comes from Pliny's *Natural History*:

Partridges fortify their retreat so well with thorns and shrubs, that it is effectually protected against beasts of prey. They make a soft bed for their eggs by burying them in the dust, but do not hatch them where they are laid: that no suspicion may arise from the fact of their being seen repeatedly about the same spot, they carry them away to some other place.

Source: Pliny the Elder, *The Natural History*. Book 10, Chapter 51. John Bostock and H.T. Riley, translators. London: H. G. Bohn, 1855.

Available online at Perseus:

<https://tinyurl.com/y8r8vp9f>.

— 5.2 —

"Occasion's bald behind." (5.2.44) — Marlowe's words.

Here is some recommended reading:

"Seizing the Occasion: How an Early Modern Emblem Changed Our Luck." Project Blog Archive. Posted by Mapping Metaphor on the 1st of November 2013. A guest post by Dr. Jennifer Craig, Wenatchee Valley College. <https://tinyurl.com/yblqn82x>.

Here is an excerpt:

When was the last time you "seized the occasion" or "grabbed the opportunity" to do what you wanted? "Seizing the occasion" brings up an image of grasping something before it passes you by, but rarely do we question exactly what we are trying to catch. The object of this metaphor is Occasio, the ancient Roman goddess of chance. In classical texts, the slippery deity is described as naked, mostly bald, and wearing a long lock of hair on the front of her head for people to catch as she rushes by, which explains the original phrase "seizing occasion by the forelock."

APPENDIX B: ABOUT THE AUTHOR

It was a dark and stormy night. Suddenly a cry rang out, and on a hot summer night in 1954, Josephine, wife of Carl Bruce, gave birth to a boy — me. Unfortunately, this young married couple allowed Reuben Saturday, Josephine's brother, to name their first-born. Reuben, aka "The Joker," decided that Bruce was a nice name, so he decided to name me Bruce Bruce. I have gone by my middle name — David — ever since.

Being named Bruce David Bruce hasn't been all bad. Bank tellers remember me very quickly, so I don't often have to show an ID. It can be fun in charades, also. When I was a counselor as a teenager at Camp Echoing Hills in Warsaw, Ohio, a fellow counselor gave the signs for "sounds like" and "two words," then she pointed to a bruise on her leg twice. Bruise Bruise? Oh yeah, Bruce Bruce is the answer!

Uncle Reuben, by the way, gave me a haircut when I was in kindergarten. He cut my hair short and shaved a small bald spot on the back of my head. My mother wouldn't let me go to school until the bald spot grew out again.

Of all my brothers and sisters (six in all), I am the only transplant to Athens, Ohio. I was born in Newark, Ohio, and have lived all around Southeastern Ohio. However, I moved to Athens to go to Ohio University and have never left.

At Ohio U, I never could make up my mind whether to major in English or Philosophy, so I got a bachelor's degree with a double major in both areas, then I added a Master of Arts degree in English and a Master of Arts degree in Philosophy. Yes, I have my MAMA degree.

Currently, and for a long time to come (I eat fruits and veggies), I am spending my retirement writing books such as *Nadia Comaneci: Perfect 10*, *The Funniest People in Dance*, *Homer's* Iliad: *A Retelling in Prose*, and *William Shakespeare's* Othello: *A Retelling in Prose*.

By the way, my sister Brenda Kennedy writes romances such as *A New Beginning* and *Shattered Dreams*.

APPENDIX C: SOME BOOKS BY DAVID BRUCE

Retellings of a Classic Work of Literature

Arden of Faversham: *A Retelling*

Ben Jonson's The Alchemist: *A Retelling*

Ben Jonson's The Arraignment, or Poetaster: *A Retelling*

Ben Jonson's Bartholomew Fair: *A Retelling*

Ben Jonson's The Case is Altered: *A Retelling*

Ben Jonson's Catiline's Conspiracy: *A Retelling*

Ben Jonson's The Devil is an Ass: *A Retelling*

Ben Jonson's Epicene: *A Retelling*

Ben Jonson's Every Man in His Humor: *A Retelling*

Ben Jonson's Every Man Out of His Humor: *A Retelling*

Ben Jonson's The Fountain of Self-Love, or Cynthia's Revels: *A Retelling*

Ben Jonson's The Magnetic Lady, or Humors Reconciled: *A Retelling*

Ben Jonson's The New Inn, or The Light Heart: *A Retelling*

Ben Jonson's Sejanus' Fall: *A Retelling*

Ben Jonson's The Staple of News: *A Retelling*

Ben Jonson's A Tale of a Tub: *A Retelling*

Ben Jonson's Volpone, or the Fox: *A Retelling*

Christopher Marlowe's Complete Plays: Retellings

Christopher Marlowe's Dido, Queen of Carthage: *A Retelling*

Christopher Marlowe's Doctor Faustus: *Retellings of the 1604 A-Text and of the 1616 B-Text*

Christopher Marlowe's Edward II: *A Retelling*

Christopher Marlowe's The Massacre at Paris: *A Retelling*

Christopher Marlowe's The Rich Jew of Malta: *A Retelling*

Christopher Marlowe's Tamburlaine, Parts 1 and 2: *Retellings*

Dante's Divine Comedy: *A Retelling in Prose*

Dante's Inferno: *A Retelling in Prose*

Dante's Purgatory: *A Retelling in Prose*

Dante's Paradise: *A Retelling in Prose*

The Famous Victories of Henry V: *A Retelling*

From the Iliad *to the* Odyssey: *A Retelling in Prose of Quintus of Smyrna's* Posthomerica

George Chapman, Ben Jonson, and John Marston's Eastward Ho! *A Retelling*

George Peele's The Arraignment of Paris: *A Retelling*

George Peele's The Battle of Alcazar: *A Retelling*

George Peele's David and Bathsheba, and the Tragedy of Absalom: *A Retelling*

George Peele's Edward I: *A Retelling*

George Peele's The Old Wives' Tale: *A Retelling*

George-a-Greene: *A Retelling*

The History of King Leir: *A Retelling*

Homer's Iliad: *A Retelling in Prose*

Homer's Odyssey: *A Retelling in Prose*

J.W. Gent.'s The Valiant Scot: *A Retelling*

Jason and the Argonauts: A Retelling in Prose of Apollonius of Rhodes' Argonautica

John Ford: Eight Plays Translated into Modern English

John Ford's The Broken Heart: *A Retelling*

John Ford's The Fancies, Chaste and Noble: *A Retelling*

John Ford's The Lady's Trial: *A Retelling*

John Ford's The Lover's Melancholy: *A Retelling*

John Ford's Love's Sacrifice: *A Retelling*

John Ford's Perkin Warbeck: *A Retelling*

John Ford's The Queen: *A Retelling*

John Ford's 'Tis Pity She's a Whore: *A Retelling*

John Lyly's Campaspe: *A Retelling*

John Lyly's Endymion, The Man in the Moon: *A Retelling*

John Lyly's Galatea: *A Retelling*

John Lyly's Love's Metamorphosis: *A Retelling*

John Lyly's Midas: *A Retelling*

John Lyly's Mother Bombie: *A Retelling*

John Lyly's Sappho and Phao: *A Retelling*

John Lyly's The Woman in the Moon: *A Retelling*

John Webster's The White Devil: *A Retelling*

King Edward III: *A Retelling*

Mankind: *A Medieval Morality Play* (A Retelling)

Margaret Cavendish's The Unnatural Tragedy: *A Retelling*

The Merry Devil of Edmonton: *A Retelling*

The Summoning of Everyman: *A Medieval Morality Play* (A Retelling)

Robert Greene's Friar Bacon and Friar Bungay: *A Retelling*

The Taming of a Shrew: *A Retelling*

Tarlton's Jests: A Retelling

Thomas Middleton's A Chaste Maid in Cheapside: *A Retelling*

Thomas Middleton's Women Beware Women: *A Retelling*

Thomas Middleton and Thomas Dekker's The Roaring Girl: *A Retelling*

Thomas Middleton and William Rowley's The Changeling: *A Retelling*

The Trojan War and Its Aftermath: Four Ancient Epic Poems

Virgil's Aeneid: *A Retelling in Prose*

William Shakespeare's 5 Late Romances: Retellings in Prose

William Shakespeare's 10 Histories: Retellings in Prose

William Shakespeare's 11 Tragedies: Retellings in Prose

William Shakespeare's 12 Comedies: Retellings in Prose

William Shakespeare's 38 Plays: Retellings in Prose
William Shakespeare's 1 Henry IV, aka Henry IV, Part 1: A Retelling in Prose
William Shakespeare's 2 Henry IV, aka Henry IV, Part 2: A Retelling in Prose
William Shakespeare's 1 Henry VI, aka Henry VI, Part 1: A Retelling in Prose
William Shakespeare's 2 Henry VI, aka Henry VI, Part 2: A Retelling in Prose
William Shakespeare's 3 Henry VI, aka Henry VI, Part 3: A Retelling in Prose
William Shakespeare's All's Well that Ends Well: A Retelling in Prose
William Shakespeare's Antony and Cleopatra: A Retelling in Prose
William Shakespeare's As You Like It: A Retelling in Prose
William Shakespeare's The Comedy of Errors: A Retelling in Prose
William Shakespeare's Coriolanus: A Retelling in Prose
William Shakespeare's Cymbeline: A Retelling in Prose
William Shakespeare's Hamlet: A Retelling in Prose
William Shakespeare's Henry V: A Retelling in Prose
William Shakespeare's Henry VIII: A Retelling in Prose
William Shakespeare's Julius Caesar: A Retelling in Prose
William Shakespeare's King John: A Retelling in Prose
William Shakespeare's King Lear: A Retelling in Prose
William Shakespeare's Love's Labor's Lost: A Retelling in Prose
William Shakespeare's Macbeth: A Retelling in Prose
William Shakespeare's Measure for Measure: A Retelling in Prose
William Shakespeare's The Merchant of Venice: A Retelling in Prose
William Shakespeare's The Merry Wives of Windsor: A Retelling in Prose
William Shakespeare's A Midsummer Night's Dream: A Retelling in Prose
William Shakespeare's Much Ado About Nothing: A Retelling in Prose
William Shakespeare's Othello: A Retelling in Prose
William Shakespeare's Pericles, Prince of Tyre: A Retelling in Prose
William Shakespeare's Richard II: A Retelling in Prose
William Shakespeare's Richard III: A Retelling in Prose
William Shakespeare's Romeo and Juliet: A Retelling in Prose
William Shakespeare's The Taming of the Shrew: A Retelling in Prose
William Shakespeare's The Tempest: A Retelling in Prose
William Shakespeare's Timon of Athens: A Retelling in Prose
William Shakespeare's Titus Andronicus: A Retelling in Prose
William Shakespeare's Troilus and Cressida: A Retelling in Prose
William Shakespeare's Twelfth Night: A Retelling in Prose
William Shakespeare's The Two Gentlemen of Verona: A Retelling in Prose
William Shakespeare's The Two Noble Kinsmen: A Retelling in Prose
William Shakespeare's The Winter's Tale: A Retelling in Prose